JACK PALMER:
A NEW ORDER

DAN BATCHELOR

CRANTHORPE
MILLNER
PUBLISHERS

First published by Cranthorpe Millner Publishers (2025)

ISBN 978-1-80378-287-4 (Paperback)

www.cranthorpemillner.com

Cranthorpe Millner Publishers

1

I've been told the human brain takes two seconds to decide how to react when receiving a new piece of information. I was about to learn this theory is false.

It was an ordinary Tuesday, the same as any other school day, and I was sitting in my Spanish classroom, trying not to lose my mind with boredom. The walls were painted white with the customary Spanish flag and map pinned up alongside 'really helpful' phrases like *Tengo catorce años/I am fourteen years old.* I was fifteen.

Of the twenty-five people in the class, at least forty percent of us weren't paying attention, but I'd lucked out with the window seat, so at least I could look out over the central courtyard, dreaming of freedom, while Mr Davies prattled on.

Of course, I was soon to learn that this was no ordinary Tuesday.

As I sat there, staring out across the grounds of the school, I ran my hands through my hair and tried my hardest to at least *look* engaged as my mind drifted to other places. My navy-blue school jumper was resting on my chair; I had made the strategic decision to be shivering but awake in my polo shirt instead of warm and asleep.

We were no more than fifteen minutes into the lesson, but it felt like fifteen hours. I didn't enjoy Spanish, and I was never very good at it. Every time I blinked, it took all my energy and focus to reopen my eyes, and as I glanced outside again, the sky seemed to perfectly reflect my mood: endless grey clouds and a light drizzle. *Great.*

Our teacher, Mr Davies, was a tall lanky man in his early thirties, with round glasses sitting on the bridge of his nose that didn't complement his long face. He wasn't the most interactive teacher – I was taking in a generous 10% of what he was saying – but when I heard him raise his voice, I decided I should probably take a break from staring out of the window.

'For the last time, David, can you stop throwing paper and focus? Do you think I can't see you? Sometimes I think you're un-teachable.'

David was my best friend; we had known each other since we started school. We both had the same love of football and trying to be funny. I wouldn't have said we were troublemakers, but we both enjoyed a good prank as well as cracking jokes (usually at each other's expense). He was slightly taller than me, with considerably broader shoulders, and wore rectangular glasses with thick black frames, alongside a cheeky grin, as if he was always up to something.

He was sitting across the classroom, after we had been separated a few weeks ago after a very intense game of dead arm. The rules were simple: see who could punch each other the hardest. To quote Mr Davies: "there are no winners to dead arm, just two losers". But, for the record, I won.

I always enjoyed waiting to see what Dave would say when he was told off; he always thought fast on his feet.

'*Arrepentido*, Señor Davies. That means "Sorry, Mr

Davies". See? If I'm un-teachable, you're doing a great job!'

'Enough!' Mr Davies chastised. 'One more peep out of you and I'll send you out for the rest of the lesson.'

Dave nodded in acknowledgment and Mr Davies continued his lecture.

I went back to staring out of the window.

I have no clue what Mr Davies was saying and writing on the board when Mrs Thomas opened the door. Tall, stern-faced, and with an abnormally large chin, the head of languages had always scared me a bit.

'Everyone leave your belongings in the classroom and head over to the sports hall, please,' she informed my half-asleep class. 'We're having an emergency assembly.'

I got out of my chair as soon as she left, delighted that we were about to miss the rest of Spanish, and headed out with the rest of my classmates.

As I was walking down the corridor, Dave came jogging over with that big cheesy grin of his, grabbing me round the shoulder.

'You got me in trouble again, mate.'

I shrugged myself out of his grip. 'How? Weren't you throwing paper?'

'Yeah, but I was trying to get your attention, arsehole. You were daydreaming again.'

I arched my eyebrows and shook my head. 'Your aim is terrible. I didn't see any paper land near me.'

Dave choked in astonishment. 'Hey, there's nothing wrong with my aim! The wind must have taken it.' His voice shifted slightly, curiosity taking over. 'So… what do you reckon this is about?'

I looked at him blankly. 'Dave, I have exactly the same

information as you. I'm just glad we get to miss class; there was a real chance of me dozing off.'

'Yeah, I saw. That's why I was trying to get your attention.' He winked. 'Just trying to be a good friend.'

I chuckled. 'You know that's a lie.' He was always trying to get me in trouble; it was like a game to him.

'Anyway, if you *had* to guess,' Dave continued, 'what would you say this assembly is going to be about?'

'I don't know.' I shrugged. 'We're probably in trouble. No one has messed around with the fire alarm recently, have they? Or started any fights?'

Dave thought for a second. 'I don't think so, we would have known if they had.'

'You never know, maybe everyone has been so well behaved we get to leave school early?'

Dave laughed. 'That's optimistic, even for you!'

I rolled my eyes as we made our way downstairs and outside into the courtyard, then towards the sports hall. There was still some drizzle, but the fresh air woke me up a little.

Spotting Amy and Laura heading over from the west wing with their own class, Dave and I waved across to them. I was surprised to see Amy – she'd been off school with flu for a while, and I could see her nose was still red from being ill.

Amy and Laura had known each other forever, but Dave and I had first met them at an athletics club, where we had formed a firm friendship. When we had all transferred to Oxford Gardens, we'd become an even tighter group.

The two of them waved back, but we didn't wait for each other; it was cold – we'd have time to catch-up later in the warm of the lunch hall.

Once we arrived in the sports hall, Dave and I squeezed onto the end of one of the many benches lining the hall. There were only a couple of rows left; it wouldn't be long until everyone was here. I noticed Amy's short blonde hair and Laura's dark, long hair a few rows ahead, their heads bobbing as they joined in with the general chatter, debating why we'd been called here at such a random time of day.

A couple of minutes passed, then the head teacher, Mrs Roberts, walked in. She was always serious and direct, but we weren't scared of her; we respected her.

The noise immediately died down.

I was regretting not picking up my jumper. I should have known it would be cold in the sports hall.

Mrs Roberts made her way to front and addressed us with a stern, 'Good afternoon.'

We collectively replied in the same monotone way as always. 'Good afternoon, Mrs Roberts.'

As she started speaking, everyone shut their mouths. If you were caught talking during assembly, you would get the death stare. No one wanted to be on the receiving end of the Mrs Roberts' death stare. It was like she had lasers in her eyes or something.

'Firstly, I apologise for taking you out of your lessons.'

No apologies needed, I thought to myself.

'About ten minutes ago, we received an official government announcement. I have called this assembly to share the information with you before it becomes leaked on social media.'

Dave and I glanced at each other; this wasn't about the fire alarms. I leant forward in anticipation.

'It has been confirmed that an intelligent alien life-force has made contact with NASA.'

I looked at Dave with a raised eyebrow, disbelieving. He wore the same expression, as did everyone else in the hall. There were a few murmurs and gasps, even laughter, but these stopped quickly as Mrs Roberts called for silence.

'At this point, there isn't much information available, but please be reassured that we are entirely safe, and should continue our daily routines as normal.' She looked at the floor for a second, a corner of her mouth lifting in a smile. 'I understand this is a lot to take in, and I appreciate you will all want to talk to each other about this, so I'm letting you start lunch break early. However, I expect you all to carry on as normal for your afternoon lessons. I understand this is an unusual announcement, but this is a day that will forever be remembered in history. Thank you for your time.'

As Mrs Roberts made her way to the exit, some of the other teachers followed.

As soon as the doors closed behind them, the room erupted in laughter and conversation. Some of our friends looked excited, some scared, others astonished. I had no idea how to react. I had gone into that assembly confident we were going to be told off, only to be informed that aliens had contacted Earth! Surely, she couldn't be serious? Aliens? That was crazy, right?

I looked at Dave. 'Well, I think it's fair to say we couldn't have guessed that.'

Dave grinned. 'I don't know about that, Jack, it would have been in my top ten guesses!'

I laughed, dismissing his comment, then looked across

the hall. We were both silent as we watched everyone else's reactions. Some people had left already, but most were still deep in conversation.

I had seen my fair share of sci-fi movies: when aliens contacted Earth, it was a lot more dramatic and catastrophic than this. In the movies, people would scream, cry, or be in complete denial. Never once had I seen a movie where people were told casually during a class assembly.

I looked to my right where Dave sat, staring at me.

'Do you believe it?' Dave asked, uncertain.

I shifted my gaze to the ceiling, gathering my thoughts. 'I guess so. I doubt NASA would release a statement unless they were sure.'

Dave looked serious. 'Good point.'

I huffed and shook my head in confusion and disbelief. 'Shall we grab our stuff and go to lunch?'

'Sure.'

It was an ordinary response to a completely out-of-the-ordinary twenty minutes.

The hall was still half-full as we left, people deep in conversation or with their heads bowed, focused on their phones.

It was only the beginning of this extraordinary Tuesday, and I didn't know it then, but that announcement would change the course of all of our lives forever.

2

We walked across the courtyard to the east wing to fetch our bags, jumpers and coats. Though the rain had stopped, the sky remained grey and it was cold outside. My coat and jumper were warm and comforting.

Everyone was either staring blankly at each other or scrolling on their phones. I doubted it would be long before people started posting their thoughts on social media about this exciting announcement (I was, at that very moment, trying to think of something witty to write myself).

After getting our belongings, we made our way to Laura's form-room, where we knew the rest of our friendship group would be. We spent most of our breaks there when it wasn't warm enough to sit outside.

I just couldn't stop thinking about the aliens. Today, the 6th of March, would be forever known as the day aliens first contacted Earth. It would be a historical event, taught in history classes around the world. Yet, right now, it seemed ridiculous.

Dave had shrugged on his football jacket, the name 'Titans' emblazoned across the back in large, bold lettering, the same team we had played for since we were little kids. I had the same jacket, but with a number five on the back instead of a three, but as we walked into Laura's warm form-room I had to take it off.

Amy and Laura were already there, sitting at the back by the windows. Laura was eating a packet of crisps; Amy, an apple.

'Hi guys!' Laura yelled energetically.

She was always excited – I didn't know how she kept it up.

'Hi,' Dave and I replied in unison, with far less enthusiasm, pulling up a couple of chairs.

'How you feeling, Amy?' I asked.

She still looked ill.

Amy pulled out a tissue and blew her bright red nose that stood out against her fair complexion and blue eyes. 'Like the weather, getting better, but still not great,' she replied with a smile.

'I bet you didn't expect to come back to hear this, did you?' Dave said as he grabbed a bottle of water from his backpack.

'No, I didn't. Crazy, isn't it?'

Laura's brown eyes lit up and she grinned from ear to ear. She was fast-talking, over-excitable and a little goofy, but she was by far the smartest in the group. 'I know! But it's so exciting! I can't wait to learn more!' She was talking loudly; we could hear the excitement in her voice.

'All right calm down or you're going to give yourself a heart attack,' Dave joked.

I looked at Amy and smirked. Though both amused, neither of us laughed.

'Anyway, we don't really know anything yet.'

Laura sat straighter and stared intensely at Dave.

He looked back without flinching.

'I know, *David*,'–she only ever called him that when she was trying to get a point across – 'but it's still exciting. People will talk about this day forever – the day we found out we are not alone – and we are lucky enough to experience it. You two are excited, aren't you?'

'Yes,' Amy said. 'I'm just too ill to show it.'

'Yeah, I guess I am,' I added, but I wasn't paying too much attention, too busy looking at my phone, reading everyone's take and posting my own: *"Can't believe aliens exist, hopefully they beam up Mr Davies"*.

I smiled to myself, happy with my work, and put my phone back in my pocket.

'Have you just posted?' Dave asked, half-looking at his phone, half-looking at me. 'Oh my god, Jack, that is *so* bad!'

I could feel my cheeks beginning to burn as the rest of the group looked down at their phones. A pathetic 'Shut up!' was the best I could come back with.

Dave was still shaking his head. 'Even my dad wouldn't laugh at that one.'

'I'd like to see *you* do better,' I sulked.

Dave pondered for a moment, then typed on his phone. 'I've done it now, check my story.'

All of us instantly looked down at our phones.

"Why are aliens so overweight? Because they eat extra-cholesterol."

Laura started laughing, Amy remained emotionless, and I put my head in my hands.

'Dave, that's way worse than mine. You criticise my post when you're writing garbage like that? Did you take that straight out of the "dad joke" book?'

'Well, *I* thought it was funny. At least mine will only be up for twenty-four hours – yours will be there forever.'

I was now definitely blushing, but thankfully, I had a slight tan all year round, which was hiding that fact nicely.

Just as I was wondering whether I should delete my attempt at a joke, the fifth and final member of our group walked into the classroom. Tom was the tallest of the group, skinny with long legs and arms that he was still growing into. He was the most serious and pessimistic of us. We'd met him when we started at Oxford Gardens; he was in some of Laura and Amy's classes.

'Tom, how bad is this joke from Jack?' Dave asked as he recounted my post.

Tom frowned, pulling up a chair. 'I saw it a second ago, and I agree, it's not very funny.'

We were all sitting round a table for two, with Laura and Amy on one side, me and Dave opposite, and Tom now perched at the head of the table.

'To be honest, guys, I don't think this is something you should be joking about. It's terrifying.'

'Oh, lighten up, Tom,' Laura said, grinning.

'But what if they're planning an invasion?'

I patted Tom on the shoulder. 'Blimey, Tom, that escalated quickly.'

'All we know is that there's been contact with Earth,' Laura added. 'They're probably billions of light years away. Relax, enjoy being part of history!'

I hadn't thought about where the aliens were... were they on a spaceship? Another planet? A moon? They probably didn't have the means to travel to Earth, though, otherwise they would have just appeared, right?

I said as much to Tom, which seemed to relax him a little, but I could see he was still nervous.

We had forty-five minutes of our extended break until we had to be back in class, so we continued to discuss the alien news, wondering what the alien had said. Just a simple 'hello', maybe? We couldn't decide, and hoped that an official transcript would be released soon. This then led to a discussion of what language we thought it would have spoken. We assumed English, but were only guessing that a decipherable conversation had taken place; it might simply have been a series of unintelligible noises.

We also discussed *how* we thought it had communicated, whether by phone or text, and then we joked about what sort of text it would have sent to earth: *Hi, Earth. This is an alien. LOL.*

Tom wasn't in the joking mood and quickly killed *that* conversation, asserting that the alien would have contacted NASA via satellite signal.

Soon, we'd exhausted the alien chat, instead discussing Amy's netball game last weekend and mine and Dave's football match. While Dave and I only played football for a local side, Amy played netball for the borough, and though none of us knew much about netball, we pretended we cared as it meant so much to Amy. She was competitive, but not conceited, so we were always happy to hear how the games had gone.

While Amy's team had won at the weekend, our football team had lost 3-1. We *always* lost. We weren't very good, though we thought we were. We always had an excuse – usually it was the referee's fault – and the last match had been no exception.

When the bell rang, we all split up. I had maths, so didn't have to walk far, but Amy, Laura and Tom had English on the first floor of the south wing, and Dave had to head back to the sports hall for PE.

The rest of the day went on like any other: everything was normal.

Normal was a good thing.

But it was impossible to know how long 'normal' would last.

3

The rain had completely cleared now, and blue sky was creeping in through the clouds, so there was no need to rush off at the end of the day. Tom, Laura and I lived on the same street, so we always walked home together. The aliens continued to be the topic of conversation. We were about five minutes from home when Tom had tried to change the topic.

'What are you two up to this evening?'

'Probably just reading about the alien contact,' I answered.

Laura nodded in agreement and the conversation returned to where it had started.

We had reached our street, a cul-de-sac, long and straight with terraced houses both sides. Laura and I lived opposite each other, midway down the road. We said goodbye to Tom, whose house we reached first. All the houses looked identical except the front doors (mine was red); each with a short drive and garden, light brown house bricks and a dark tiled roof.

After saying bye to Laura, I opened my front door and went into the kitchen, pouring myself a glass of orange juice. I was the only person in, as my dad was picking my nine-year-old sister, Claire, from karate.

Taking the glass to my bedroom, I dropped my bag by

the door and took off my coat, throwing it on the double bed, obscuring the crumpled duvet. A window in the far wall overlooked the back garden; I had a desk with old pieces of homework thrown across it, my laptop hidden beneath. I considered my room tidy, but my parents begged to differ.

I put my glass on the bedside table, grabbed my laptop, and jumped on the bed, my back resting against the wall. With my legs outstretched, I turned on the laptop, ready to investigate.

I knew every news website would feature reports of the aliens, though much of it sensationalised. I wanted facts, and thought NASA's website would be the best place to start.

Their site was easy to navigate; the lead story easy to find. In large writing at the top of the home page was the tagline: *The First Encounter*. Next to it was a photograph of a white-haired man in his sixties, with a white beard and thin, round glasses. His name was Dr Griffiths, the author of the article. I sat forward and read:

I manage the satellites at the NASA base in Houston and can confirm that an extraterrestrial has communicated with NASA, at 5:00 a.m. local time. The extraterrestrial used one of the satellite signals that we send to outer space. I was the first to receive contact; it greeted me with: "Hello". I was more than a little startled and surprised, but cautiously replied "Hello" in response. The voice was very flat, modulated and robotic, inhuman, yet it spoke English. It went on to ask how I was; I replied, though astonished.

I then asked who it was. It said it was from a planet two hundred light years away (over two thousand trillion kilometres). It told me it meant us no harm, assuring me it was not violent and we had nothing to fear. Like Earth, its planet is also the only one inhabited in its solar system. The planet's inhabitants are a much older species than humans; technology far more advanced than the human brain could comprehend. As a species, it searches for life across the universe.

We are not the first, nor the last life form it hopes to find.

It told us we should consider it male, and call him Professor Watson (the human name it had chosen). It called itself the leader of the Earth team. Apparently, there are different teams following and studying different planets. The Earth team has been studying and learning about Earth for hundreds of years, learning our different languages and history, this is how it knew about NASA and to address me in English. They have studied every detail: the way we socialise, our technology, our wildlife, and our own space program and how we have progressed.

They learn about a planet and then decide when it is ready to be contacted. It can be a very short period of assessment; sometimes contact is never made. Over the last few human years, it has debated when our planet would be ready to be told there was life beyond Earth.

They decided we are now ready.

He concluded that he was aware this was a

momentous day for mankind and did not want to divulge too much, too soon. He would be in contact again over the next couple of days. He then thanked me for my time before ending contact.

There is much excitement at NASA; for many years, this is something we have been hoping for. As soon as we have any further information, we will report it immediately.

I hope you all feel the same way as Professor Watson and I: we are ready.

I sat back, stunned. It was hard to believe what I had just read; it didn't seem real. I reflected on the phrase *"we are ready"*, recalling how everyone at school had reacted to the news. Everyone had been surprised, but continued with their normal daily routine. What else could we do?

Maybe we were ready?

That was without mentioning the fact this species had searched for, and found, other aliens before us. Everything we normal people understand about the universe and life could all be wrong. Just like how many ancient cultures believed the Sun orbited Earth and were proven wrong. This was just another thing human beings were wrong about.

That night, I was sitting at the dinner table with Claire and my parents, enjoying the Shepherd's Pie Mum had made that morning. She looked tired; it must have been a tough day at the hospital. I wondered if she'd had any crazy people coming in, terrified about the aliens.

'See, kids, I told you, didn't I? You're both aliens, but

you never believed me,' Dad joked in his booming voice.

I had inherited the same round, cheeky face as his. He could make a joke out of anything (I got my sense of humour from him; I always had a comeback, too).

'Guess you were right all along. Do you reckon they'll finally take me away from here?'

Mum chuckled at our antics. She had an easy-going nature and didn't like conflict. 'Come on, you two, play nice.'

'Sorry, love, we're only having a laugh. So… are you two feeling alright about all this?' Dad asked.

Claire had been particularly quiet all evening. 'What if they want to destroy the planet?' she murmured.

I laughed; it reminded me of what Tom said earlier. Mum kicked me under the table, trying to keep the peace.

'They won't destroy the planet,' Dad said reassuringly. 'What about you, Jack?'

I shrugged nonchalantly. 'It doesn't scare me.' I turned to Claire. 'They don't want to hurt us – the alien told the NASA scientists it wouldn't. Besides, if the aliens really wanted to, they would have done so years ago.'

Claire looked more relaxed. 'Why are they only contacting us now?'

'I don't know, but I guess we'll find out soon enough. I wouldn't worry. I mean, if *we* had the technology to communicate with other planets, we probably would. Or maybe it lied, and it *is* dangerous. Perhaps they eat human brains! Then we'd be in real trouble!'

Claire left the table and ran up to her room. *Dammit.* I'd just been messing around. She was more afraid than I had guessed.

'Wait, Claire!' Mum shouted, trying to get her to stop. She glared at me. 'That wasn't nice, Jack.'

I looked over at Dad guiltily. I hadn't meant to upset her.

'You have to remember she's only nine, Jack. Besides, you don't want to upset your mum and sister – even aliens aren't as scary as them when they're grumpy!'

Grateful to my dad for his support, I helped him clear the table before going upstairs to apologise to Claire. By now, she had calmed down, embarrassed by her reaction. Usually she enjoyed joking around. Though Claire didn't add to my stupid jokes, she was always the first to laugh. I told her fear was nothing to be embarrassed about. I couldn't blame her for being worried; it was a scary thing, knowing there was something else out there more powerful than us.

I realised I was being selfish joking about it; lots of people were going to be afraid and I needed to accept that. This was the biggest thing to ever happen to mankind; it was to be expected that people would react differently.

That night, I lay in bed with my hands crossed behind my head, staring at the ceiling, thinking about everything that had happened. That alien life existed was mind-blowing.

Before falling asleep, I lay in bed for hours contemplating everything. My mind kept returning to Claire's question.

"What if they want to destroy the planet?"

4

Beep, beep, beep. My alarm went off at 7:00 a.m.

I am not a morning person.

The painful noise of the alarm always cut through my head and I quickly turned it off and lay on my back, inhaling deeply. I rubbed my face to try to wake myself up, and wiped the sleep out of my eyes with my fingertips. I took a sip of water from the glass on my bedside table and sluggishly planted my feet on the floor. Leaning forward, I rubbed my face again before circling my arms, feeling every muscle in my body stretch. I groaned with the effort of undertaking my customary morning ritual.

Just as I was about to jump in the shower, I heard my phone vibrating. I picked it up and saw Amy's smiling face on the screen with her hair pulled up in her trademark ponytail. That was weird. We never spoke in the morning.

I stared at the screen for a second, debating whether to answer. I felt like a zombie and was not in the mood to chat. Of course, after a moment I decided I was better off knowing whatever she wanted to tell me.

'Hello?' I grumbled hoarsely.

'Hey, how are you?' she asked.

I inhaled another deep breath before puffing out my cheeks as I exhaled a few seconds later. 'I'm fine, I think. I'm not really with it yet. What's up?'

'Sorry, I know it's early. I didn't sleep much. I wanted to talk to you last night, but I got so caught up reading everything online it would have been too late.'

'Some would argue now is too early.' I leant back on my bed, my feet still rooted to the floor. 'Everything okay?'

'Yeah, I just wanted to ask if you read up on the alien last night.'

'Of course I did.'

'So you know it's found life on other planets?'

'Yep.' I continued to rub my eyes, trying to focus on what she was saying.

'Isn't that insane?'

'Yeah, I guess.'

I had thought about it while lying in bed last night, thinking it crazy that, before yesterday, we'd assumed Earth was the only planet with intelligent life. But I was still too sleepy to discuss it all now with Amy, knowing we would be having this same conversation throughout the day anyway. Amy and I always had similar views, and I enjoyed having these kinds of conversations with her, but not at 7:00 a.m. (I enjoyed very little at 7:00 a.m.).

'I'm not sure what to think. It all just seems a bit much. This discovery will change everything, won't it?' She sounded genuinely concerned and I suspected she had been up all night worrying about it.

'Don't worry, I doubt it'll really change anything. I mean, sure it will change the way everyone thinks, of course it will, but our day-to-day will stay the same. Doubt they'll let us skip out on school now that they know there's life out there, you know?'

'I suppose…' She sounded unconvinced. 'Anyway, sorry for calling so early. I'll see you in a bit. Thanks for making me feel better, you always know what to say.'

'No worries, glad I could help.'

The rest of my morning schedule went ahead with no further delays. I showered, changed into my uniform and went downstairs to grab a bowl of cereal, which I ate on the living room sofa while watching *The Breakfast Show* on the large flat-screen TV and scrolling on my phone. It wasn't usually interesting, but I was a creature of habit and this was part of my morning routine. At least today I knew I would be more interested in what they were reporting.

The male and female presenters (yes, I fancied her, that was the only reason I watched the show – sue me) were discussing Professor Watson's message. I learned nothing new; most of the headlines were predictable, or recycled film and song quotes. Another newspaper had reported that a bald, slightly overweight man had locked himself to the gates of Buckingham Palace, with a large cardboard sign round his neck that read: *The end of mankind.*

This type of dramatic reaction didn't really surprise me, and I was sure it wouldn't be long before at least a few more extremists declared the end of the world. He was just another person seeking his fifteen minutes of fame.

According to the presenters, the mood across the world was largely very positive. Global street parties had been held, and footage showed some of them, with guests dressed as famous movie characters including the alien from *Toy Story* and Spock from *Star Trek.*

It was fascinating really, how some people feared the

news while others embraced it.

At this point, I didn't feel strongly either way. I always liked to think things through logically, and I never panicked unless I felt there was something to panic about. So, I panicked when I forgot to do my science homework, because I knew I'd be in trouble, and that scared me (the teacher was terrifying). But right now, I merely found the alien interesting, and a crazy guy tying himself to a palace gate wasn't going to change that.

I had lost track of time, now running a few minutes late. I quickly ran to the kitchen and put my bowl in the sink, leaving it for someone else to wash. I always walked to school, and so just before 8:00 a.m., I grabbed my coat and set off.

The blue sky was welcome after all the recent rain, a metaphor for the mood of the nation, I hoped. It was one of those mornings when it was chilly in the shade but warm in the sun. Jogging down the road, I met Tom and Laura outside Tom's house.

'Did any of you guys read up about Professor Watson?' Laura giggled as she said it; she clearly found it funny calling the alien by a human name.

'I did. Hilarious that the alien seems to have more manners than most of our year group.'

Laura and I shared a grin at Tom's characteristically sarcastic comment. He had a dry sense of humour, and occasionally delivered a good one-liner, but it was hard to tell if he was trying to be funny or just being himself.

'I know! Who would have thought the first would be so friendly,' Laura replied.

'At least he doesn't seem threatening,' Tom added.

'What about the other planets?' I asked, interested to hear their thoughts before we saw Amy.

Tom and Laura normally had strong opinions on most things, especially Laura; if you didn't agree with her, she would continue trying to convince you until you did (or *said* you did). I had learnt to agree from the outset. Tom, meanwhile, usually dismissed others' opinions if he thought he was right, or simply refrained from asking what others thought.

Laura was first to reply to my question, speaking rapidly. 'I thought about it, but decided it was no big deal. I mean, whether it's one, two, or a hundred different types of alien life, what does it matter? He reassured us he wasn't violent or wanting to hurt anyone.' She paused to gasp for breath. 'There is going to be *so* much to learn from the professor.'

I smiled and nodded in agreement. I liked the nickname "The Professor".

'I agree with Laura,' Tom said. 'Obviously I'm still sceptical, but I don't think we have any reason to fear.'

My eyes widened in surprise. His response was uncharacteristically laid back, *and* he'd agreed with Laura (normally the two of them were like two heavy weight boxers going at it).

'I really thought you would be more freaked out about this.'

'Well, I'm not. I did a lot reading about it all last night and, at the moment, it all seems okay.' Tom then went on to reference the guy who'd chained himself to the gates of Buckingham Palace. 'What a joker; I don't know how extraterrestrials consider us to be intelligent life-forms with people like that representing us!'

Tom was on a roll this morning. It was good to see him revert to his normal disapproving ways; it had caught me off guard that the news hadn't made him more fearful.

I looked to the skies and shook my head, unable to think of a reply to his observation.

At school, we went straight to Laura's form-room to relax before the start of the day, sitting together at a table by the window. A couple of minutes passed before Amy walked in and sat next to me. Despite her lack of sleep, she didn't look tired. In fact, she looked better and healthier than yesterday, now without a red nose.

Dave was nowhere to be seen, but that wasn't a surprise. Every day he arrived within a minute of the bell. I could never understand why he always agreed to meet us when he knew he would only have a minute to chat before going again. But that was classic Dave; he'd never change.

On cue, Dave walked in. 'Alright, guys,' he said cheerfully, the bell ringing at the same time.

Dave's shoulders drooped as if this didn't happen every morning.

Groaning with annoyance he reopened the door and said, 'Bye, guys,' before walking straight back out again.

None of us had the same lesson on a Wednesday morning, so we all said bye to each other and went our separate ways.

Just before Amy walked off, I grabbed her gently by the forearm and turned her around.

'Are you okay?' I whispered, not wanting other people

to hear.

She smiled. 'Yeah, I'm good. Sorry about calling, I was being silly – over-thinking stuff. But you were right, everything is just the same.'

'You can call me anytime, about anything. Just maybe not at 7:00 a.m. if you want me to actually respond.'

Amy chuckled. 'Thanks. I'll try to avoid calling so early.'

We smiled briefly at each other before heading to our lessons.

The rest of the day passed by uneventfully, as did the rest of the week. No further supposedly non-existent creatures were discovered; we didn't find out that the Loch Ness Monster or the Abominable Snowman existed, nor that Big Foot lived among us. All such supposed Earth-dwellers were of minuscule importance, however, compared to alien life.

No further news was released about the alien species, other than gossip pieces. People waited in anticipation to discover facts, hoping for an official announcement. We knew Professor Watson would be in touch with NASA soon. It was a waiting game.

Everyone could sense something big was building, we just didn't know what.

It wasn't until the weekend that we learned more.

5

On Saturday mornings, I played football for the "mighty" Titans, meaning I got to leave the house wearing one of the coolest kits in the league: orange socks, black shorts, and a long-sleeved orange shirt featuring the club's logo of a Spartan helmet and the team's name written below in capital letters. Despite our awesome kit, our team was one of the worst performing teams in the league. We might have looked like the Dutch, but we didn't play like them.

Dave's dad, Peter, was picking me up that morning. He was a mountain of a man, and an intimidating sight to any stranger, but I knew he shared the same cheerful approach to life as his son. Some parents made me feel awkward, but I could chat to Peter like he was one of my friends.

'Morning! Thanks for picking me up,' I said enthusiastically as I jumped into the car. I was in a good mood, looking forward to playing football.

'Hey, Palmer.' He always called me by my surname. 'How are you feeling this morning?'

'I'm good, thank you, looking forward to the game. Think we have a chance of winning today.' I was feeling positive, but it was usually false optimism.

Peter laughed, over-exaggerating the sound for comic effect. 'You never know, miracles could happen! Just like that alien.'

Dave turned round and rolled his eyes, dismissing his father's jokes, as usual. 'Funny and topical, Dad. I'm surprised you know about it, since you never watch the news.' His eyes sparkled with mischief, goading his dad to react.

'Watch what you say, son, or you'll be walking home.'

Dave winked at me in victory, the rest of the journey continuing in the same light-hearted manner.

We predictably went on to lose the football match against The Lions; in a week full of surprises, our loss wasn't one of them. We were dreadful, but that didn't bother us – neither Dave nor I were competitive, we just enjoyed playing (if that was what you could call it). Excuses for our losses were a given; we knew it was no one else's fault, but it seemed easier to blame anyone but ourselves, much the same way as in class when the teacher told us off and we would instinctively point to the person next to us.

'I still can't get over how badly the ref did today,' Dave groaned on our way home. 'Every week we get bad decisions.'

'I know. We get nothing but bad luck. One of these weeks a decision will go our way though, I'm sure of it.'

Peter laughed. 'You boys must be from a different planet if you really think the ref had anything to do with your losing.'

'Please, Dad, for the last time, stop making alien jokes. They weren't funny yesterday or the day before, and they still aren't funny today,' Dave snapped.

His tone was always less jocular after a football defeat.

'All right, son, calm down. Don't get moody with me

just because you lot keep losing every week.'

Checkmate: Peter. Dave may have won the conversation on the way to the match, but Peter had got the better of him on the way home.

Once we got back, I thanked Peter for the lift and let myself into the house, using the key beneath the welcome mat. I walked to the kitchen for a drink, thirsty from playing football. The dining room door was ajar and I could see Dad at the table, reading the newspaper with a cup beside him, steam rising from it. He heard me come in but didn't look up.

'Did you win?' he called out, though he already knew the answer.

'No.'

'What was the score?'

'3-1. The ref's fault.'

I grabbed my glass of water and a snack and went to eat it in front of the television.

'Thought you'd want to watch this,' Dad said, picking up the remote control.

'Oh yeah? What is it?' I asked through my mouthful of food.

'Dr Griffiths released a new statement about the alien. Thought you'd be interested.'

He brought up a video of the statement. Dr Griffiths was seated at a wooden desk, a white wall behind him. His beard looked as though it had been trimmed and his hair neatly brushed with a side parting. I could see he was talking to a roomful of people, perhaps a load of journalists. The wide camera angle suddenly zoomed in closer, Dr Griffiths taking up the whole screen.

He sounded nervous as he began to speak, a slight tremble in his voice, but he spoke slowly and coherently. He was staring down the camera with a focus in his eye that suggested he was reading off an autocue.

'Over the last couple of days, a small group of specialists and I have been in discussions with Professor Watson, trying to learn more about him and his species. He has so far been very co-operative and has answered all our questions.

'Firstly, I would like to assure people this is no hoax. I understand there will be sceptics, but we have quantifiable evidence to support everything we have so far been told. Professor Watson contacted us for a second time, saying he realised we would have a lot of questions, and that he would do his best to answer, but didn't want to overwhelm us with too much information all at once.

'We began by asking about his species, and were told they come from a planet a hundred and twenty times bigger than Earth. They are the dominant species on their heavily populated planet. Water exists there, though they do not need it to survive. They also have oxygen, but interestingly they do not need it. They have discovered further life forms in other galaxies, some that do require oxygen to breathe, but others, not.

'They have lived on their planet for over fifty billion human years, and their average life expectancy is seven hundred. Professor Watson is four-hundred-and-eighty-two. They only began searching for life on other planets a million years ago. He understood that to us this might seem like a very long time, but that we should understand their planet has a much older history than ours. Science is very important to them, which is what started their project.

'His vision is for humans and his species to regularly connect with one another, so that we can begin to view them as something other than an "alien" species. To respect his wishes, NASA chose to replace the word alien with "Elder", in recognition of their advanced years in comparison to humans.

'His final request was that global leaders should gather to talk to him as one. The meeting is scheduled to take place next Wednesday at 2:00 p.m. Eastern Standard Time. I will not be taking any questions at this time as I have nothing further to add. NASA will release another statement as soon as we have anything more to communicate.'

Dr Griffiths moved to leave and the camera angle widened again. Lights began flashing as the press took photographs.

Dad and I had sat in silence throughout the short press conference, giving it our full attention. We were transfixed; an Elder could have walked into the room and sat next to me and I wouldn't have noticed.

Dad paused the TV and looked at me questioningly. I looked back at him and shrugged my shoulders, unsure what to say. I felt confused. I didn't know what to make of the press conference; I thought it was a bit of an anti-climax. It still felt strange to talk about Professor Watson so casually.

'It was a bit disappointing,' I said.

'I agree. I thought we would learn more than we did,

though I do agree it's sensible to drip-feed the information to stop people freaking out.'

'Why do you think they want to meet world leaders?' I thought it a peculiar way to end the conference.

Dad scratched his chin, deep in thought. 'Probably just to discuss more about the Elder, and for him to learn more about us.' He shrugged. 'I don't know, your guess is as good as mine.'

'If they are going to talk to humans, I guess it makes sense for it to be the people in charge.'

We switched to the sports channel to get the latest news before matches began. And just like that, the conversation moved on. Though this was the biggest thing to happen to mankind, we still wanted to know the starting line-up of the day's matches.

It had been a crazy couple of days, but as Mrs Roberts had said, we should continue life as normal, and that's exactly what I intended on doing. Right now, I wanted to watch Saturday afternoon football. There would be plenty of time to talk about aliens over the coming days.

The weekend went by uneventfully. While I spent Saturday afternoon horizontal on the sofa, Dad played a round of golf (poorly) and Mum and Claire went to the cinema. Afterwards, we had our customary take-away pizza for dinner, much to my delight.

I had intended spending Saturday evening in a similar lazy manner, but Dave called and changed my plans. He was like a cat, only giving you attention when you ignored him. He had bought a new video game, which, funnily enough, involved being attacked by aliens, and begged me to play it with him. Mum chauffeured me to his house, a ten-minute drive-away. I ended up sleeping over in the spare bedroom and Peter dropped me back the next day.

I spent Sunday being lazy, and before I knew it, another weekend had passed and I was back at school.

However, this hadn't been an ordinary weekend. It had been the first time I'd heard the term "Elder", and I knew it wouldn't be long until even more information was discovered… for better or worse.

6

When I arrived at school on Monday morning with Tom and Laura, Rob Brown was standing outside the main entrance, looking shifty. Rob was in the year above and always wore a long black coat and black baseball cap, whatever the weather. He was the only person at school who was never told off for wearing a cap; we never knew why.

I didn't talk to him that often, but I always made sure to say hello when I saw him. I didn't want to get on his bad side.

'Morning, Rob!' Laura said enthusiastically (even on a Monday morning, she had the energy of an excitable puppy).

'Morning, guys,' Rob responded in his usual monotone. 'Any of you want to put a bet on how many arms the alien has?'

Rob saw himself as the school's bookie, and was always trying to get people to make bets. He would either grow up to be a shrewd businessman or lose all his money gambling.

His question got me thinking. How strange that we had known about the alien for nearly a week, yet still had no idea what it looked like.

'What's the highest number of arms someone has guessed?' asked Tom.

'Twenty-seven.'

'Someone bet on it having an odd number of arms?'

'Yesss,' replied Rob slowly, as if Tom was asking a stupid question.

Tom laughed, covering his mouth with his hands. 'That's one of the most ridiculous things I've ever heard! Why would someone bet on an odd number when limbs always come in pairs? Even bugs have an even number.'

He was acting like a know-it-all, as usual, but I had to admit that his point was valid.

Laura wacked him on the arm. 'Oh, shut up, Tom! We don't even know if it *has* arms. Until a week ago, we didn't even know it existed! It's not completely unreasonable for someone to guess an odd number. The aliens' norm may be completely different from ours; they might think it's funny we have an *even* number of arms. It's just a bit of fun, anyway. People can guess what they like.'

'Someone actually bet on no arms,' Rob added.

Tom's eyes widened. 'Who?'

'Sorry, I can't disclose that information. Client confidentiality and all that.'

Rob might be an idiot, but no one could say he wasn't professional; he took his betting very seriously.

Putting his hands in his pockets, he walked into the distance without saying goodbye. At least he'd given us an interesting start to the morning.

The rest of Monday and the following day passed at a snail's pace. Everyone was waiting for the next big announcement on Wednesday. It felt like the lead-up to Christmas when time went incredibly slowly, the days before always mundane and boring.

It was impossible to focus on school or anything else when such a big statement was due. NASA's previous report hadn't been very exciting, and I was hoping to learn something completely unbelievable this time. After talking to Rob on Monday, I was crossing my fingers that we might even discover what the Elders looked like.

Wednesday finally came and excitement levels were at fever pitch. It wasn't every day that there was a genuine possibility of seeing an alien. While the original announcement had come out of the blue, this time the build-up was massive. We had to wait until 7:00 p.m. Greenwich Mean Time before we'd know the outcome of the world leaders' talk.

We were restless all day, concentration at an all-time low. The teachers didn't even seem to mind, equally as excited. I just hoped all this commotion was worth it.

Seconds felt like hours during last period, but finally, the day was over. At home, I changed into a pair of jeans and a hoodie before jogging up the road to Tom's. We'd all decided to order pizza and watch the announcement together.

Sandra, Tom's mum, opened the door. She was always cheerful, the complete opposite to Tom, and immediately ushered me inside.

'Come in, come in, Laura's already here. We're still waiting for David and Amy. Are you excited?' she asked, moving out of the way to let me in.

I slipped my shoes off then put them neatly on the shoe rack. 'I am. All this build-up has been keeping us on edge.

Are you?'

She smiled. 'Very. It's such a monumental moment. None of it has seemed real until now. This time it's really sunk in'

Sandra took me into the living room where Tom and Laura were sitting on the sofa. On the TV, a team of scientists and celebrities talked about the imminent announcement, considering what might be discussed and its possible effect on Earth and its future. The segment was just filling time; it was a cross between the punditry of football and the news. We weren't really watching, too busy discussing everything among ourselves, and trying to keep Laura from bouncing off the walls in anticipation.

At 6:00 p.m. Dave and Amy joined us in the living room. We chatted for a while and ordered pizza, tucking in hungrily as we waited to hear what the discussions between the Elder and the world leaders had been about. Time slowed down again as we sat there. I knew the meeting could go on for hours, and it would be some time before any news was released.

I still felt excited, but had used up far too much of my energy eating, and I wasn't the only one. Dave was lying in the middle of the living room on his back like a starfish; Laura and Amy were sharing the larger sofa and had their heads against opposite arm rests; Tom was lying across the smaller sofa, and I was sitting on the floor next to Dave, legs outstretched and leaning backwards on my forearms. It wasn't our finest hour.

'My stomach hurts so much; I don't know how much more I can take,' Dave said dramatically. Anyone would think he had been *forced* to eat so much. 'How much longer?'

'Please, David, stop moaning. We could be waiting hours before we know anything,' Amy grumbled.

'But what if it's still another two hours? I don't know if I can hack it, Amy,' Dave whined.

I'm not sure how Amy would have responded, but she didn't have to, as at that moment the image on the TV showed the same conference room where Dr Griffiths had made his last statement. This time, Dr Griffiths was accompanied by a colleague and they both sat behind the desk.

Tom turned up the volume. We were all completely silent as we sat up to listen.

'Good evening,' Dr Griffiths said. 'This is my colleague and close friend, Dr Jackson. He has worked closely with Professor Watson and acted as the bridge between the professor and world leaders, who arrived earlier. He will be reading the statement.'

The new person looked younger than Dr Griffiths; he had a thin body and face, and wore a stereotypical long, white laboratory jacket.

'I know some of you might be slightly surprised that the meeting was so brief,' he said, 'but the purpose of the meeting was not to enter into further discussions but to plan next steps.

'Professor Watson has confirmed that the Elders have a means of travelling through space, which is far more sophisticated than ours. Their resources are far superior; they can travel though space in the same way we travel around the world. He didn't go into any further details other than to state that their technology is very different to ours, and at this stage, we lack the knowledge to understand it. He went on to say that this assertion was not meant to intimidate us, or in any way appear arrogant, but just to let us know that they have the technology to reach Earth.

'The world leaders and scientists present at the meeting unanimously and enthusiastically agreed to the visit. For the professor's safety, the meeting will take place in an undisclosed location at an undisclosed time. All I can confirm is that it will take place within the next week, after which another statement will be released.

I lay down and stared up at the ceiling. Though the press conference had been brief, it had certainly lived up to the hype. An alien was about to come to Earth!

Dave spoke first. 'I like the sound of this Professor Watson. He seems like a stand-up guy… or alien, rather.'

Dave was joking, but from what we knew about Professor Watson, he did seem to be a "stand-up guy". I had never put much thought into it, but I suppose I had always assumed that when an alien first visited Earth, it would be spontaneous. I certainly didn't think they would be asking permission and arranging a date!

'He is polite, isn't he?' Amy agreed. 'This is happening ridiculously fast, though. We've only known of their existence for a week and now they are coming to Earth.'

Tom decided it was his turn to speak. It was never long before it was Tom's turn. '*Too* fast, Amy. We should be doing extensive background checks. We can't just invite anything to Earth. We don't even know his motives.'

'Tom, relax,' Laura told him, 'he *has* asked permission to visit. If he planned to hurt us, I doubt he would have taken the time to ask for an invite.'

They had both made interesting points, but how did someone do a background check on an alien? If they had the technology to travel through space, surely we were not match against them? If they wanted to invade us, they could.

7

The next few days passed by with the usual routines, but there was a noticeable nervous tension in the air. Everyone seemed a little more on edge; people didn't like the uncertainty of the visit. It felt like we'd all gone to the cinema and there'd been a power cut halfway through the film. We didn't yet know how the film would end.

We hadn't been told when or where the visit was taking place, or what would be discussed. I knew everyone would feel much easier once an announcement had been made.

Meanwhile, we still had to go to school, and my parents still had to work; people were still going about their daily routines. The majority were open-minded about the visit, though, and eager to learn more.

The idea of the Elders existing started to feel more real with each passing day, rather than just being a weird news story. However, what had begun as excitement for me, had now been overshadowed by a cloud of uncertainty, and a lot of people seemed to be feeling the same. Something didn't feel quite right, but it was difficult to explain.

A couple of days later, I was sitting with Claire after school, watching the news, which wasn't normally my nine-year-old sister's favourite show. Mum and Dad were both still at work, then heading out for dinner afterwards, so I had agreed to look after her. I was hoping to find out what was happening with the Elder, but the news reported a riot taking place in Mexico. People were angry, protesting about Professor Watson's visit. Police were shown trying to stop the protestors by any means necessary. There must have been over five hundred people marching, screaming and chanting, which made me wish I had tried harder during my Spanish lessons so I could understand what they were saying. It looked serious, many of them being beaten and dragged away by the police.

Once the news report started showing people screaming, crying, and dripping with blood, I immediately switched it over. It didn't make for easy watching, and Claire didn't need those kinds of images in her head.

It was the first time I had understood that not everyone welcomed Professor Watson's visit, and that unfortunately, humans could be violent.

Glancing at Claire, I realised she was sitting bolt upright, staring at the TV, like she was in some kind of trance. I nudged her shoulder, snapping her out of it, and she looked up.

I smiled hesitantly. 'Are you okay?'

She thought for a second; she was clearly nervous. 'What if there's a war?' She averted her gaze, looking uncomfortable. It was a dramatic thought, but it wasn't uncommon for her to jump to the worst-case scenario.

'Why do you think there's going to be a war, Claire?'

'Because of what we just saw!'

I nudged her again to make her look at me. 'Don't worry about that. That was people all the way on the other side of the planet. It would be the same if we protested at school: it might be newsworthy, but it's not going to change anything. Like when Mum tells me off – I can argue and protest as much as I like, but I'm never going to change her mind.' I tried to say it with confidence, to make her believe me.

'So, it won't stop the alien coming?'

'No. Besides, for all we know, he may already be here. Trust me, in six months' time, this will all seem normal.' For once, I was trying to be the supportive big brother, knowing this time making a joke of it all wasn't going to cheer up Claire.

'I hope so. I don't want anyone to get hurt.'

'You've heard the interviews – Professor Watson won't hurt anyone. He's nicer than me, isn't he?'

Claire smiled and sat back. She did look slightly more relaxed now. 'Maybe.'

We spent the next couple of hours watching cartoons and messing around. If a statement about the visit was going to be released, I would have to wait until Claire had gone to bed to find out what it was about. Taking Claire's mind off everything was more important right now.

In general, the people I knew were welcoming the idea of Professor Watson's visit. I had never stopped to think that some people would be unhappy, violently unhappy, like those protestors in Mexico. It had clearly been worrying Claire and I was sure she wasn't the only one.

I started to question whether I was excited or scared. Everything *could* change. But then, all big ideas or significant moments divided opinion. For me, despite the sceptics, I decided his visit was still a good thing.

Days passed and we received no further news regarding the visit. Every day we thought a statement would be released, but when more than a week went by, it started to seem like it might never happen.

I spent my time as normal, going to school and hanging out with my friends. On this particular evening, I was with Dave. We were lying on the sofas watching TV in comfortable silence. When we were in a group, neither of us would stop talking, both always fighting to be the centre of attention, but when it was just the two of us, we often sat in comfortable silence, enjoying each other's company without the need to talk.

When we did finally speak, for once the alien was not the topic of conversation. Instead, we talked about Laura, who had a date with a guy from school tonight. His name was Mark Newman, and he was annoyingly handsome; popular with the girls. Neither Dave nor I liked him, finding him bland. We didn't think he would be Laura's type, though we didn't really know what that was.

'He's a drip,' Dave said. 'And she always has a million things to say. I can't imagine what the conversation will be like.'

I laughed. 'Well, lots of crazy stuff is happening these days. To be fair, we hardly know him. He might be okay.'

'Nah, the guy's a dry wall. He has zero personality. He'll regret asking her out anyway, she's just going to bend his ear about the Elders.'

I was surprised by how bothered Dave seemed by the whole thing. He certainly hadn't been this bothered about the aliens.

Dave hadn't taken his eyes off his phone the whole time we'd been talking, so I was startled when he sat upright at the speed of light.

'What is it?' I asked, sitting up too.

'I was just checking the headlines on NASA's website, and guess what the main headline is?'

'What? Is it about Professor Watson's visit?'

'*Unveiling of Alien Next Week,*' Dave read the headline. 'Come on, put the news on.'

I grabbed the controller from the floor and immediately switched to the news channel.

A news reporter in a grey suit was sitting behind a glass desk, a red wall behind him. He had a piece of paper in front of him and was already speaking when we tuned it.

'… a statement has been released by Dr Griffiths regarding the historic visit, which we can confirm has now taken place. Professor Watson arrived on Earth in a small ship. A full description of the ship has yet to be revealed, but we are hoping a picture will be released imminently.

'Dr Griffiths began by describing Professor Watson, although the description may not be accurate as we have learned the Elders have the technology to shape shift. Dr Griffiths went on to say that the Elders developed this ability when they began looking for life-forms beyond their own planet. They understand that when they visit other planets, it is often the first time the inhabitants will have seen an alien species. They want to make the experience as stress-free as possible, so they shift into a familiar form to aid acceptance. What is familiar varies from planet to planet, so they conduct extensive research to make sure it is correct each time. Professor Watson said that, over time, he hoped to teach us about other planets and the life they have discovered, but it is important that we take slow steps at this early stage.

'Dr Griffiths described Professor Watson as being very tall – around 7ft – with an elongated body. He referred to him as a humanoid being with visible skeletal structure, though lacking muscle definition. His arms were disproportionate to his body and slightly longer than a human's, and there were three long fingers and a thumb on each hand, four toes on each foot. His skin was smooth and grey. His head appeared in proportion to his body but with no hair and no noticeable nose or ears, only small orifices in their place. His mouth was small, and his large, black opaque eyes had no pupils.'

The Elders had clearly done their homework – it sounded like Professor Watson looked exactly like a human would expect; an alien straight from a Hollywood movie!

'He greeted everyone with a handshake and then the meeting began. From the beginning, Professor Watson made his intentions clear: he wants to reveal himself to earthlings and broadcast his statement live on television. He said it will take years of learning about them before humans will be able to accept and understand them, so he wants everyone to be involved as early as possible.

'I can now confirm this global broadcast will take place next Saturday in Madison Square Garden, New York, at

8:00 p.m. Greenwich Mean Time in front of a live audience of scientists and politicians. Dr Griffiths concluded that Professor Watson intends to talk about his species in great detail so that we can all learn more.'

I glanced curiously at Dave; he was perfectly still, a blank look on his face. We were both waiting, it seemed, for the other to talk; make the first move like in an old-fashioned western shootout.

I finally relented. 'So, an alien is going to be on TV next week.'

We both processed this in silence for a moment.

'Apparently so.' He was in shock, as was I.

'So, what will you be watching next Saturday night?' I asked, trying to inject humour into the conversation, encouraging Dave to respond.

He shook his head and ran a hand across his face, as if trying to rub some life back into it. 'I don't know. Is there any football on?'

We both laughed awkwardly.

'I wonder why they really disguise themselves?' Dave pondered, frowning.

I shrugged. 'Didn't the reporter say something about it making us feel more comfortable?'

Dave looked at me as if I was an idiot. 'Come on, mate. Aliens are coming to Earth, a disguise would hardly make us feel more comfortable!'

I shrugged again. 'I don't know, *David*. Maybe they're actually a foot tall and they do it to look more intimidating.'

'If they were disguising themselves to look more intimidating, surely they wouldn't tell us they were in a disguise?'

I shrugged my shoulders for a third and final time. 'What is this, twenty questions? I don't know. Why would they lie to us? If they want to make themselves look different, let them. Some questions are just unanswerable, like why you are always late to school yet still insist on meeting us first.'

Dave looked offended. 'I'm not *always* late.' He changed the subject. 'I want to see his spaceship.'

I nodded. 'Well, I'm sure we will soon enough.'

We then continued to watch TV while both updating our stories. Dave lazily recycled his earlier joke: *"Does anyone know if there's any football on next Saturday night?"*

I went with: *"I hope Professor Watson's parking is better than my mum's."*

The weekend passed with no new information on the alien, but plenty of speculation. We played football and added yet another defeat to our less than impressive record. Other than that, the weekend passed by uneventfully, watching TV and films at home. I even decided to break the habit of a lifetime and do some homework. It felt like everything was changing, but also nothing at all.

I was looking forward to Monday. I wasn't particularly excited by the thought of school (even though, for once, I had done my homework), but I was looking forward to chatting to my classmates about Professor Watson. For thousands of years, humans had been the apex species on Earth, but as of Saturday, we were welcoming a far more advanced creature to our planet.

It felt like everything was about to change.

8

I got ready as normal and met Tom and Laura at the end of the road on Monday morning. When we arrived at school, we found that Dave and Amy were already waiting for us. My jaw almost hit the floor. I couldn't believe Dave was on time! It was the first time this had ever happened.

I didn't know what my face had looked like when we were told aliens existed, but it couldn't have been as shocked as the expression I wore now.

'What are you doing here?'

Dave looked around, then at me, eyes wide. 'What do you mean? I do go to school here as well, you know?'

'Yeah, but you're never here on time. Is this because of what I said on Friday?'

Dave shook his head, dismissing me. 'How was your date, Laura?' he asked, not so subtly.

Dave was never the smoothest, but it was all starting to make sense.

'It went well. We got on much better than I thought. We have a lot in common, and he's really funny,' Laura said, cheerfully.

Dave's face reddened; I had never seen him look so vulnerable.

'So, do you think you'll go out with him again?' Dave asked.

Laura smiled and shrugged. 'Nothing's been decided but I hope so.'

Amy and I looked at each other – she was as confused as me. Luckily for Dave, she didn't want to make the situation any more awkward than it already was, so she changed the topic.

'What does everyone think of Professor Watson appearing on TV?'

'I'm so excited!' Laura squealed. 'When Mark told me, I didn't believe him, so I checked for myself. It's going to be amazing!'

Dave didn't say anything. He looked awkward and sullen, aggravated that Laura had mentioned Mark.

Tom had a stern expression on his face. 'It's certainly not ideal that an alien is here on Earth. That said, I am fascinated to see it. Although I have no idea why it isn't showing us what it really looks like.'

Amy nodded. 'I am slightly anxious about him being here, but I'm excited to see him. The disguise thing is weird, though.'

'Maybe he's ugly?' Dave suggested, attempting a smile.

He wasn't succeeding.

Laura shrugged. 'I guess he'll talk about his reasons on Saturday night.'

The bell sounded and everyone started to make their way to class.

Amy stopped me in the corridor. 'What's going on with Dave?'

'I've got no idea, why?'

She gave me a look. 'Okay... why is he being so funny

about Laura, then?'

I shrugged; I didn't really want to be having this conversation. 'I don't know. He hasn't said anything to me. I'm sure he'll talk to us if he wants to. I wouldn't over-think it.' I didn't want to betray his confidence. If Dave wanted to tell everyone, he would; I wasn't going to be the one to bring it up. I'd never enjoyed gossip.

'Well, I hope he doesn't carry on acting weird,' Amy said as she started walking to class.

'It's Dave, he's always weird!'

The morning passed relatively uneventfully, though it seemed everyone was on high alert. Teachers didn't even try to stop us checking our phones. In fact, I caught a few of them doing just that whenever they could.

During our lunch break, a photo of the spaceship was released. Tom brought our attention to it, his hands shaking as he held up his phone.

Dave snatched the phone out of Tom's hands and stared at the image. 'That's pretty cool!'

I took the phone from Dave and studied the picture. The thin spaceship looked to be no longer than ten metres, its shape not dissimilar to a Formula One car. It was metallic and silver, with wings on both sides, and no visible engines, like you'd expect to see on a plane. It wasn't particularly impressive.

'It doesn't look like I thought it would,' I said, passing the phone back to Tom.

'What do you mean?' Tom asked.

'It looks too small and simply constructed. I thought it would have a massive engine or jets on the wings or something more high-tech.'

'Why?'

I rolled my eyes at Dave. 'Because it travels through space, duh!'

'They did say their technology is very different to ours, so it makes sense. They probably think it's funny that we need such big rockets to get ships into space,' Tom suggested.

Once again, Tom had made a good point. I shouldn't have been surprised that the ship looked completely different to what I had expected.

'Do you think we'll learn more about their science and technology on Saturday?' I asked him.

'Doubt it. It's probably far too advanced for our brains.'

'Well, maybe *your* brain, Jack!' Dave joked, wearing his trademark cheesy grin.

'Shut up, Dave. If they're not going to teach us about their way of doing things, why are they here?'

'I guess we'll find out on Saturday,' Tom replied.

The rest of the week passed by incredibly slowly. I wasn't sure if the week had been any more boring than any other, or if it was just because I was counting down the days until Saturday. Everything felt mundane in comparison. We had learnt so much over the last couple of weeks – some of it difficult to believe – and now we would finally see Professor Watson.

There was only one topic of conversation to be heard

everywhere. More photos of the spaceship were revealed from lots of different angles. There were no sharp edges, the body of the ship was a perfect curve. The back arched away into a point that couldn't be seen in the first photos released. It looked like a futuristic concept car. I still had no idea how it flew. As far as I could see, there was no engine.

Like the rest of the world, Dave became focused on Saturday, and finally started acting normal again, though I had a feeling it was only a matter of time before weird Dave returned… especially since Laura and Mark were due to go on a second date.

9

After weeks of reading gossip, keeping up with the news and watching experts discuss the Elders, Saturday had finally arrived.

There was no football match, but I still woke up early, filled with anticipation. I couldn't wait to see Professor Watson for myself. The thought had kept me awake for most of the night, but I wasn't tired; I knew adrenaline would get me through the day.

I grabbed my phone from the bedside table, wanting (like every morning) to see if there had been any further announcements and gauge the general feeling around the world. I went on various news websites, and every report was upbeat, any former pessimism now forgotten (or covered up).

The broadcast later that night was being hailed as the greatest moment in human history; one that would unite the world. Even alone in my room, I could feel the sense of expectation in the air.

I made my way downstairs for breakfast, taking a bowl of cereal and a glass of orange juice into the living room to watch TV. Claire was already there, sipping a glass of milk.

'What's up,' I croaked, sitting beside her on the sofa. 'Are you looking forward to later?'

Claire took a big gulp of milk, then put the glass on the

floor. 'Mm-hm. I wonder what he'll say.'

I swallowed some cereal before responding. 'I'm not sure, maybe he'll sing to us! Nothing surprises me anymore. All I know is that it's the greatest discovery mankind has ever made.' I was on the Elder bandwagon now.

'No, it isn't. We didn't discover them.'

I looked at her, puzzled. 'What do you mean?'

'Well, *they* discovered *us*.'

I didn't like being outsmarted by my younger sister – why'd she have to be so damn clever?

I went back to staring at the TV, casually replying, 'That's what I meant.'

The news reporters showcased the build-up, with footage of parties and huge screens being erected in readiness for people to flock to the streets to watch it together.

In an effort to keep busy before the broadcast that night, Amy, Dave and I decided to meet in town to go bowling. Both Tom and Laura were visiting their grandparents. We hadn't been bowling in what felt like years, but it seemed like a good activity to help pass the day quickly.

I caught the bus to the bowling alley. It was a cold but bright day and everyone on the bus was in a noticeably positive mood. It seemed everyone was out and about, though maybe they were also trying to distract themselves from thinking about Professor Watson's appearance later.

When I eventually arrived at the bowling alley five minutes late – the bus had taken forever – Amy was already there. She was always on time, unlike Dave, for whom we had to wait a further fifteen minutes. When he eventually joined us, I thought he looked surprisingly fashionable, for him at least. There were lots of people about and there was a carnival mood in the air. Almost everyone seemed to be in good spirits. If there was any negative feeling towards the upcoming broadcast, I didn't spot it.

Though maybe I was just naïve.

Of course, Dave won both our games, and I came last – both times. Though we only played for fun, it was never fun losing in such spectacular fashion, especially when Dave was the one bragging about his victories. I wouldn't have minded so much if Amy had won.

'Today is going to be a great day. I've demolished both of you clowns at bowling and later I get to see a real-life alien!' Dave grinned like a hyena.

Amy kicked him under the table good-naturedly. 'Shut up, David! You got lucky. I was just getting into the swing of things.'

'Yeah, me too,' I murmured.

Dave looked at me in disbelief. 'Jack, you were terrible. We could have been there all week and you still would have lost every game!'

'Are you joking? I 100% would have won the third game. I was getting better; I only *just* lost to Amy in that second game.'

The day had grown colder while we'd been holed up indoors, and it was beginning to get dark by the time I waved Amy and Dave off.

'See you tomorrow! Enjoy tonight,' Dave said as their bus pulled up.

'I'll call you after the broadcast,' Amy added.

The bus doors shut, and they waved back at me as it

sped away, knowing that when we next saw each other, everything would be different.

While I waited for my own bus, my thoughts returned to Professor Watson. I could barely stand still. I had always been fascinated by groundbreaking events of the past, but I had never thought I would be lucky enough to witness an event of such magnitude, let alone experience my very own sci-fi movie.

In a few hours, Professor Watson, an alien, would be on live television, and the whole world would witness history.

10

'I hope you're hungry,' Mum said, stirring the pot of chilli con carne on the hob as I walked through the door.

'It smells amazing. What time are we eating?'

'Another hour,' Dad said, looking up at me from washing a chopping board in the sink as I grabbed a can of lemonade from the fridge. 'That gives us enough time to eat then watch the build-up afterwards.'

'Sounds good to me.'

'Your sister's in the living room watching TV. Why don't you join her? We'll give you a shout when it's ready.'

I smiled at Claire as I walked into the living room, and she smiled back. The TV showed Madison Square Garden packed full of people; it seemed every scientist and politician in the world had been invited.

Hundreds of reporters had flocked there as well and were interviewing guests as they arrived. Everyone was saying the same thing: how happy and grateful they were to be there and what an honour it was.

Claire and I watched until dinner was ready – early for once. We began eating hungrily, everyone enjoying the food too much to stop to talk, as well as wanting to rush back to the TV.

Finally, Mum asked Claire and I if we were both looking forward to seeing Professor Watson.

'Yeah, but it's going to be so weird,' I said. 'The food's amazing by the way, Mum.'

Claire nodded, but looked nervous.

Dad looked over at her. 'You have nothing to be scared of, Claire. He will just say a few words, then things will go back to normal. It will be exciting to see an alien, won't it?'

Claire smiled at him. 'I guess.'

Soon, she would see she had nothing to be afraid of.

'How was bowling?' Dad asked me.

'It was fun, thanks, made a nice change. Dave was really good.'

'How was Amy?' Mum added.

'She was good too. I was the worst by a mile,' I said, smiling. It hadn't *actually* bothered me, but I knew Dad would still make some cheeky comment to goad me.

'Well, that's not a surprise to anyone.'

I nudged him with my elbow but chose not to comment. I didn't want to bite too hard, bringing attention to my lack of sporting ability.

'Well, Amy is really good at sport anyway, so I'm not surprised she was better than you,' Mum said, trying to offer motherly support but only shining a light on my shortcomings.

Dad and Claire both laughed and I could feel myself blushing with embarrassment.

'What's that supposed to mean?'

'Nothing, just that Amy's good at sport. You're good too, she's just better,' Mum replied cheekily.

It was the most backhanded compliment I had ever heard from her. Though Mum came across as being kind and quiet, she had the same mischievous sense of humour as the rest of us.

Defensively, I tried to convince them that bowling wasn't really a sport, more a hobby, but they weren't converted.

It was strange to be less than ninety minutes away from seeing Professor Watson and not be talking about him. Though I supposed there wasn't much left to talk about; it was all we had spoken about for weeks. Now we were just trying to kill time; have fun, at my expense.

At 7:00 p.m. we left the table and took our plates into the kitchen, where Mum and Dad washed up. By 7:30 p.m. we were all sitting in the living room, Mum on the small sofa, Dad and Claire were on the larger one. I was sitting cross-legged on the floor, staring at the TV. With less than thirty minutes to go, we were all focused on the main event and conversation had stopped.

The presenters informed us that there were over fifteen thousand leading politicians and scientists in Madison Square Garden, all currently facing the stage, waiting for Professor Watson's appearance. The only thing on the spotlit stage was a white lectern in the centre, NASA's logo clearly visible. There didn't need to be anything else; what was about to happen would be epic enough.

With ten minutes to go, a timeline of recent events leading up to this moment flashed across the screen, and at 7:55 p.m. the stage camera zoomed out. It was obvious something was about to happen.

Moments later, Dr Griffiths walked onto the stage from the right-hand side. He was wearing a smart black suit with a white shirt and red tie. This was the smartest we had seen him. He stood behind the lectern, which hid the bottom half of his body. As he began to speak, I could hear his voice trembling. With the world's press watching, the event being televised globally and fifteen thousand eminent people present, it made sense he would be nervous. Not to mention the fact that the place was eerily silent. It was like the world was holding its breath.

'This is a story that has gripped the nation,' he began. 'And one that is by no means reaching its conclusion. This is just the beginning. I'm sure all of you here today, indeed everyone around the world watching, have many questions. How could you not? This is unprecedented, unfathomable, and how lucky we all are to be present at this moment in history that will change life as we know it forever. I cannot answer your questions, but there is a being here today who can. He is what you have all been waiting for. And so, all that is left for me to do is extend a very warm, and human, welcome… to Professor Watson.'

The camera zoomed out again as Dr Griffiths looked to his left, and the crowd started applauding emphatically. I knelt up, the excitement pouring out of me, my family all leaning forward too in anticipation. The atmosphere inside our living room was electric, even without the crowd of people.

Then, finally, it happened.

First, a long shadow appeared on the stage, a dark silhouette that clearly belonged to an imposing figure, before a tall dark shape filled the spotlight. Professor Watson was standing there in his entirety: tall, confident and proud. He was exactly how Dr Griffiths had described;

he looked like a stereotypical "Hollywood alien". The camera zoomed in on the top half of his body and I could see he looked exactly as I had pictured, though I hadn't expected him to be wearing a sharp black suit, white shirt and black tie, and be waving at the camera.

Dad laughed. 'I can't believe he's wearing a suit!'

Mum shook her head and shushed him. This wasn't the time to be making jokes, although it was a fair point.

The camera angle continued to pan so the whole stage could be seen as Professor Watson made his way to the lectern. He took long, lazy strides but walked exactly like a human. Dr Griffiths was waiting for him, and when Professor Watson stood next to the doctor I realised how tall the alien was – more than a foot taller.

They shook hands and then Dr Griffiths left the stage, the camera now focused solely on Professor Watson.

Professor Watson began to speak. I wasn't sure if it was his voice, or because I was concentrating more than I ever had before, but he was hypnotic. Though he spoke in a monotone, robotic voice, like Dr Griffiths had described, there was a noticeable friendliness and familiarity there too.

'Greetings Earthlings. Firstly, I would like to take this opportunity to thank everybody for taking such an interest in me and my species. I would also like to thank NASA for their co-operation and hospitality. Their kindness has reaffirmed why we were so interested in visiting this great planet.'

The camera angle widened to capture the whole stage again. Though Professor Watson continued talking, I stopped taking in what he was saying as another man had walked onto the stage. He was dressed in baggy old jeans and a dirty, red-checked shirt. He looked old and worn out, with long, messy grey hair and a scraggly beard. He didn't look like a scientist or politician. He was walking like a man possessed, directly towards Professor Watson, who hadn't appeared to notice him. That was, until people in the audience made a sound of warning and Professor Watson turned and looked directly at him.

The man pulled something out his pocket and pointed it at Professor Watson.

Bang!

The noise echoed around the room, followed by a deathly silence.

Then, Professor Watson fell to the floor with a heavy, dull thump.

11

What followed was the most terrifying and surreal experience of my life. The assassin was taken down immediately, and the stage was flooded by guards and officials. Chaos reigned.

Not long after that, the live broadcast was cut, our television showing a technical failure screen. I always tried to be calm in a crisis, not that I had ever been in one like this before, but this time I felt things getting on top of me almost instantaneously. Any excitement I had felt was gone. I could feel the panic rushing over me; the butterflies in my stomach were no longer the good kind. My heart was racing at a hundred miles per hour, my palms were sweating, and my eyes wide open as adrenaline shot through my body. I was acutely tuned in to all my senses. I was petrified – not like horror-movie scared – I feared for my life. I felt sick, I couldn't sit still, and I was looking around as if I would find an answer somewhere. I couldn't understand what I had just witnessed. Why would someone assassinate Professor Watson? What did this mean for Earth?

Were we going to find out who that man was and why he had done it? In many ways, I realised, as fear engulfed me, it didn't matter. It was done, and there would be consequences for humankind. Terrifying consequences.

I looked over at Mum, her hands on her head, clearly

in shock. Dad's face was expressionless. He didn't seem to know how to react to what he had just seen.

Up to this point, although everything had been very weird, for some reason it had felt believable and under control. It didn't feel like that anymore. I felt like I had been ready for anything that night, but not this. Claire had started crying hysterically and she couldn't catch her breath. I thought she was going to vomit. Dad hugged her, rubbing her back, trying to calm her down as she cried into his chest. He didn't say anything though; there was nothing he could say. I could see Mum's eyes starting to tear up and it made me want to cry. If I hadn't already known how serious the consequences were going to be, I did now by my family's reactions. For a second, I wondered how every other household in the world was reacting.

I didn't know what was going to happen to Earth. Up to now, everything had felt like it was being managed, as if some of what would happen would be on our terms. Now, I felt like we had just lost that privilege. I couldn't believe one man had changed everyone's future.

My head started pounding the more I thought about it. It was the uncertainty that was making me panic. This was going to end disastrously. My breathing began to speed up; I thought I might be having an anxiety attack.

I took a deep breath and swallowed. 'What just happened, Dad?'

He let out a shaky breath. 'I don't know, Jack.'

It was the answer I was expecting, but not the one I wanted. 'But what do you think is going to happen?'

'I don't know,' he said again.

He sounded as scared as I felt.

The TV flicked back to the conference. It had only been about two minutes since the gunshot was fired. The live stream was back on and all we could see was the stage and what looked like medics surrounding Professor Watson and the man who had shot him.

I didn't know what they were expecting to do, but before I even had a second to think, the ground began to shake. Not like an earthquake, but as if the whole world had moved. All the power went out and we were left in total darkness.

There was silence for a few seconds, before Claire burst into tears again. It seemed louder than before, now that it was the only noise in the room. Dad tried to calm her, but she wouldn't stop. My heart was racing faster than ever, so fast I thought it was going to beat out of my chest. I stood slowly, my hands shaking. What I couldn't work out was why we were in total darkness. I didn't know the exact time, but it couldn't have been any later than 8:30 p.m. It shouldn't have been pitch-black, not at the end of March. I had never experienced darkness like this.

I put my hands out in front of me. I couldn't see, but I knew the room well, so edged myself slowly and steadily towards the window, my arms outstretched in front of me to make sure I didn't walk into anything.

I gently pulled the curtains aside so I could see out the window, but my eyes hadn't adjusted to the gloom at all.

'Where are you, Jack?' Mum called out to me.

I could hear the worry in her voice.

'I'm by the window, Mum, don't worry,' I whispered. I

couldn't pinpoint the reason why I was talking so quietly, but it seemed like the sensible thing to do.

'Why? Come here,' she whispered back.

'One second.' I was looking up and down the street, but all I could see was darkness. The sky was completely black as far as the eye could see. It didn't make sense – it had been a nice day, the sky had been clear; there should still be light. Even if it was just a freak evening of early darkness, I should still be able to see at least one star, but it was as if something was covering the sky, something that went on for miles.

It was no coincidence that Professor Watson had been shot and then straight afterwards we were plunged into total darkness. Something terrible was about to happen.

Just as I started to edge away from the window, the streetlights flickered on. I blinked a few times to adjust my eyes. The light was creeping into the house, and I turned round to see all my family looking at me.

At least we had each other.

'Dad, come here.'

He made his way to the window and stood next to me, looking out at the sky.

'What is it?'

'Look at the sky, why is there no light?' I whispered.

'I don't know,' he whispered back.

We didn't want to scare Claire or Mum. We could hear both of them crying.

'There's something in the sky.'

Dad didn't reply, he didn't need to.

We stood a little longer, looking up. Suddenly, large

circles started appearing, all over the sky, as far as the eye could see, making them impossible to count. Whatever it was blocking the sky, it was massive. Blinding white lights shone from the circles, and I had to squint to look at them. They were like massive spotlights shining onto the floor. Dad and I looked at each other, confused and frightened. The nearest spotlight was at the beginning of our road. Things then began floating down from each one. Whatever they were, there were hundreds, coming now in a constant flow. As they got closer to the ground, I was able to make out aliens in the same form as Professor Watson. I could only see their silhouettes, but each one was identical to our recently deceased visitor.

Dad grabbed my arm and dragged me away from the window.

'Everyone, follow me, now,' he ordered.

Mum grabbed Claire's hand and met us by the living room door. We were all standing close together. Dad put his hands on mine and Claire's shoulders.

'Whatever happens next, I want you to know I love you both and won't let anything happen to you.' Dad sounded confident despite the odds being against us.

'I know, Dad.' I replied. 'I love you too.'

I could feel my eyes watering. I knew Dad would do anything he could to protect us, but I also knew he was powerless to stop what was happening. It wasn't going to end well. Claire nodded and continued to cry as she embraced Dad. We stood for a few seconds looking at each other before Dad told us to follow him.

We were about to make our way upstairs when suddenly

the front door burst open.

In front of an orange glow, a silhouette appeared. It was one of the Elders. I couldn't discern any features, but this certainly was not a human. Everyone screamed in shock, fear and disbelief. The alien crouched to step into the house, and we all ran upstairs and locked ourselves in the bathroom. I knew it was only a matter of seconds before it got through the bathroom door. There was no thought process, just fear. It was human nature to run from trouble, and that was exactly what we had done.

We were crouched in the middle of the bathroom, embracing each other, staring at the door. Claire was crying, and I could hear Mum and Dad's shaky, fearful breathing. I was staring at the door through watering eyes, my head and heart pounding. I was overwhelmed by emotion and just wanted to scream; for everything to go back to normal.

I was certain I was about to die.

The door burst open again, but this time, we had nowhere to run to. The alien stood before us. Despite the poor lighting from the single window, I could see it clearly. There was a silver ball in its left hand no bigger than a tennis ball, the meagre light coming in through the window bouncing off it.

The alien slowly began to lift its left hand and pointed the ball towards us. At the same time, Claire slipped away and ran straight past the alien and down the stairs. Mum and Dad both screamed Claire's name. I couldn't see Claire now, but I could still hear her loud cries, the sound growing fainter the further away she ran.

The alien turned round, its left arm outstretched, facing

towards the stairs. A red laser came shooting out of the ball in the direction Claire was running. The laser lit up the whole house for a split second, then darkness followed and total silence.

There was no longer any sound of crying.

Before I had a chance to register what had just happened, Dad stood and started running towards the alien, letting out a loud war cry as if he was running into battle. Before he had a chance to strike at the alien, it turned and shot the laser again. The room lit up, the laser hitting Dad.

Instantly, he was gone.

Only then did the realisation hit me. I wouldn't be seeing my little sister or Dad again.

I sat there in Mum's embrace, listening to her weeping. It was horrific. I could see the alien. All my senses were working. But I wasn't taking anything in. Tears were streaming down my face, but I couldn't feel myself crying. I felt numb, a pit in my stomach that felt never ending. My heart felt like it had been shredded.

Claire and Dad had disappeared within seconds. Seconds. It was no time at all.

My brain wasn't working; it was like I was having an out of body experience. I was looking at myself, broken. I was no longer Jack Palmer.

I could feel myself standing up. I wasn't thinking, but I knew what I was going to do. I was going to kill the alien that had done this to my family.

Just as I had begun to stand, I felt Mum squeeze my arm.

Through the tears, I heard her whisper, 'I just lost your

father and sister, I'm not losing you.'

I fell to my knees, sobbing uncontrollably. I had never felt worse. I looked at Mum and she looked at me. This was the end. The alien stood with his left arm outstretched, pointing the ball towards us. I looked at it, expecting a laser to shoot out and for us to share the same fate as Dad and Claire. Instead, the ball started glowing with a bright white light. It was hypnotising. I did my best to look away and stay awake, but I was powerless to it.

Before I knew it, I was unconscious.

12

When I awoke, I ached everywhere and my head felt ready to explode, the headache was so bad. I felt as though I had been asleep for days. With a dry mouth and a thumping head, I realised I could have been. For a moment, I thought I had awoken from a bad dream, but that was too good to be true. As my senses began to return, I quickly began to worry about what else had happened while I was unconscious. Then I decided I didn't want to know.

It was still dark except for the blindingly bright, circular lights coming from the sky. I was outside, and had been placed on my knees. It was cold and I could see my breath. I was afraid for my life.

Mum was to my left and had also just begun to wake up. The relief was overwhelming, and I looked up to the sky in gratitude. I didn't know what I would have done if she wasn't there.

Looking to my right, I spotted an unconscious man I didn't recognise. I looked around and there were thousands of people everywhere, all on their knees. That's when I noticed the buildings around me.

We were in the school courtyard.

We were lined up in perfect rows, all facing the sports hall, as if attending a concert. By this point, so much had already happened that nothing felt real anymore. I was exhausted and just wanted it to be over, but I knew we were far from the end.

Looking around again, I noticed the aliens surrounding the courtyard, watching us like security guards at this haunted concert we had all been brought to. Mum and I were towards the east wing near the back, and I could see a few of the aliens clearly. Glancing up at the buildings, I saw more of them. All the windows were smashed, the aliens inside, presumably in case they needed to shoot at us. There was no chance of anyone escaping.

A few minutes passed, and nothing happened. I could hear a few mutters, but most were too afraid to talk, or else in shock. Mum and I kept glancing at each other, but we never said a word. Finally, an alien walked out and stood in front of the sports hall. We were so far away, it was almost impossible to see anything except that the ball it was holding, which glowed bright red, the only light in the yard.

Just as I thought the alien was about to speak, a man a few metres in front of me stood and sprinted to his left. He was shouting as he jumped over people, trying to escape. His courage was admirable and internally I was willing him on, but in an instant, he was hit by a red laser and disappeared. The shot had come from behind me. I could instantly feel the hysteria among the crowd; the sheer terror. People started crying, most of them staring at the floor, desperate not to attract any unwanted attention. I didn't react, simply taking in the obvious warning.

There was no escape.

The alien at the front began speaking. Though it wasn't

holding a microphone, I could hear every word clearly without it having to strain its voice. It sounded exactly like Professor Watson.

'Our leader came to your planet to teach and develop you as a species, in the same way we have educated other planets. We meant you no harm, we are not evil, nor violent, and we will not attack unprovoked. When one of your kind shot and killed our leader, that was an act of war. We have been left with no choice but to retaliate.'

The alien was speaking slowly and clearly, non-threateningly. There were no awkward pauses; he must have prepared what he was going to say. Everyone was silent, a mixture of fear and concentration.

The alien continued. 'We outnumber you; our science is greater than yours, and we know your planet better than you do yourselves. If you are waiting for a response from your leaders, I can tell you now not to bother. The army bases you had have already been destroyed. You cannot fight.

'Any human still alive will be listening to a speech like this one; every human across the world has been gathered to a public space like this and told their future. As I previously said, we are not an evil nor violent species, but we will do what is required to avenge our own and to educate your species, by any means necessary. We are now your leaders, and you will obey our instructions. If you obey, you will survive. If you do not, there will be fatalities.

'The first instruction is to sit and wait while we gather the names of everyone here. You will then be divided into groups and an elder will take you somewhere in the building to rest. After a short while, you will come back outside, in groups. At intervals, there will be a holographic wall for you to look at. On this wall will be your name. We will give you time to look through them so you can determine who in the area has survived. There were many fatalities during the last five hours, and I am sure you will all want to know if your loved ones have survived. After this, your elder will give you further instructions. Please sit quietly while we take your names. Do not give us a reason to shoot.'

I sat, unable to think. Fear does that to you. There had been no war, yet within one night, we had lost our planet, our home, our families. It had been done easily and effortlessly. We had just been gathered up like animals and told to follow instructions.

In the movies, when aliens invaded, it always looked like a fair fight. We would always fight back and regain our planet, even if we were the underdogs. That wasn't going to happen in reality. I hadn't expected it to be so brutally efficient.

Yet… no humans *had* to be killed. They were keeping us alive for a reason. To study us, maybe? All we had been told was that they would only kill those who openly defied them.

I didn't know what the future would hold. All I knew was that Claire and Dad's names would not be on the wall; that Earth was no longer a place we could call our own.

I continued to sit on my knees, staring blankly at the ground. My mind was empty, my body weak. Everything I thought about brought nothing but despair. At this point,

I wasn't even grateful to be alive; everything just seemed hopeless. All sense of time had disappeared, and I had no idea what was going on around me. I was mentally exhausted, yet for some bizarre reason I didn't feel tired; the idea of sleeping again didn't seem like a possibility.

I sensed it before I saw it: an alien towering over me. It looked the same as every other alien I had seen; there was nothing to distinguish them from each other. Its large, deep, black eyes showed my reflection, but I didn't recognise the person looking back at me. I looked so helpless.

'Name?' it asked it the monotone voice I knew I would have to get used to.

'Jack.' I cleared my throat to try to get myself out of the trance-like state I was in. 'Jack Palmer.'

The alien continued to look down at me and I continued to stare into its eyes. It didn't say anything and moved dismissively to the person next to me.

'Name?' I heard it say again, and again. It had a job to do.

I could feel myself getting agitated and angry. Being that close to an alien without retaliating, after everything that had happened, felt wrong. I tried to focus on my breathing to clear my mind, but I was just getting angrier. My senses were returning and I had become acutely aware of everything. There was a chance I was having a panic attack and an even bigger chance I was going to do something extremely stupid, or dangerous. Mum squeezed my hand; perhaps she could sense my restlessness. Either way, her reassurance helped. Out of the corner of my eye, I saw groups around the edge of the courtyard being taken away by Elders. I looked at Mum and she smiled at me, as if to say "don't worry". But we both knew it wouldn't be long until we were moved on.

Mum and I and thirty or so others were taken away and guided by a single alien. We followed in silence to the south wing of the school, to Laura's form-room. The alien told us to wait there. I sat at the rear of the classroom with my back against the wall. It has been on my mind ever since we arrived at the school yard, but for the first time I allowed myself to consider what had happened to the rest of my friends. Nobody in the room was talking; everybody was thinking the same thing, but nobody knew what to say.

As the night went on, the silence eerie as we waited, my back slid further down the wall. My eyes were becoming heavy; I felt emotionally and physically drained. Every time I felt myself falling asleep, I would suddenly wake myself up. Keeping my eyes open was becoming more of a battle, but I didn't want to sleep. There was too much going on for that.

A new order had begun.

13

'Everybody, follow me.'

I woke up suddenly; I must have drifted off. I didn't know how long I had been asleep for. I looked around and wiped my face. Whatever had been blocking the sky (I assumed a spaceship) had now moved and daylight was shining through the windows. Picking myself up off the floor, I stood with Mum. We were all taken outside the same way we had been brought in. As promised, a holographic wall stretched from one end of the courtyard to the other. It was three times taller than me and had rows of names all the way across. The wall glowed a mint green colour that I could see through. All the survivors' names from our area were written in black capital letters. I walked along the wall with Mum; the surnames were in alphabetical order.

People on the other side of the wall were also checking to see if family and friends had survived. Some people were embracing one another and looking relieved. Others broke down; too many people were not seeing the names they were hoping for. It wasn't easy, but we went straight to P, even though we knew exactly what we would see. There I was, J. Palmer, and Mum, S. Palmer. But no T or C. Palmer. I already knew, of course. I had seen Dad disappear and heard Claire's cries stop as she was shot at from the bathroom. We shouldn't have put ourselves through it again.

We stood for a few seconds, staring at the names, but nothing changed. There were still two missing Palmers.

I cleared my throat and looked at Mum, my voice croaky. It had been a long time since I had spoken. 'I'm going to go see if any of my friends survived.'

'Okay.' Mum's voice wobbled, and I could tell she was trying not to cry again.

'I'll be back in a second.' She nodded at me as I walked along the wall.

I thought about the aliens. After everything that had happened, it was strange to think they would let us check for survivors, the act almost human. I couldn't understand their motives. It was too much to think about. As I checked the wall for my friends' names, my heart began racing again and I became increasingly nervous. I went to R first, as it was the nearest.

I scanned my eyes up and down and breathed a sigh of relief. There it was: A. Reed. Even after everything that had happened, this felt like a small victory. It wasn't over yet though. I walked further up the wall to S, looking through all the names, but there was no L. Scott. The feeling of victory passed quickly. I felt sick, and it occurred to me how unfair it was. Out of everyone, she was the most excited about the visit.

I didn't stay for long – I couldn't bear the thought of not being able to see my friend again – and began looking for more names. I got to T, panicking and praying that Dave's name was on the wall.

There it was: D. Thomas.

I smiled, I was so pleased to read his name. If only I could see him. The happy feeling was fleeting as I finally walked back to find C, discovering there was no T. Casey. He had been right to be afraid. It didn't feel real. Though Tom and Laura's names weren't there, I couldn't believe I would never see them again. I didn't want to believe it.

As I walked back to meet Mum, it suddenly occurred to me that Tom and Laura had been visiting grandparents that day. There was a chance they could be on a wall somewhere else. It was a long-shot, but I had to hope it could be true.

Mum gave me an enquiring look.

'Amy and David were on the wall but no Tom or Laura. But they were away visiting their grandparents so they may be okay.'

'Hopefully.'

We joined the rest of our group at the end of the wall and walked back to the room that had been allocated to our group. I sat against the wall again, resting my head back, my elbows on my knees. Why had they let us see the names of the survivors? I couldn't understand what they were trying to achieve. It was still hard to believe any of this was happening, or what was next, but I knew it wasn't going to be good.

Life as we knew it was now in the balance and we had to try and survive each day as it came.

14

Months had passed, and we were still sleeping in the same classroom. The Elders had quickly given us a routine and every day was the same. Times and dates were irrelevant now; our only calendar was the marks on the wall some of our group had made to keep track of the days. I no longer knew if it was a Monday or a Thursday, nor what the time was, and I didn't care either; it didn't change anything. We just did as we were told.

Every day started with an early wake-up call from an Elder. Our Elder called himself Commander Wilson, and he was strict. It was impossible to know how strict in comparison to others, as they all looked and sounded the same. The only mark to differentiate between them was the armband they wore. Commander Wilson wore a red armband with the letters CW in large white writing. I'd never had a conversation with him. In fact, I'd never seen *any* human have a conversation with him.

After the wake-up call, we had two minutes to get outside and line up in our classes. We would stand one behind each other in neat rows along the courtyard, our elder standing at the front. Our commander would then walk us outside the school grounds in a perfect line. Every group would leave through the main gate – we were one of the furthest away from the gate, so had to wait for most of the others to leave first.

The streets were now mainly rubble. I can still remember the first time I saw them; it had felt so weird. It was impossible to believe that there were once houses standing there. The natural landmarks like trees and bushes were unharmed, but anything man-made had been destroyed. Human history and culture had been deleted; we were now living on the Elders' planet.

They had left remnants of some buildings as well as things we could build with, though it all just looked like concrete and rock to me. All we did, all day, every day, was build. We weren't told what we were building, we just did as we were told. The buildings were rectangular and of a similar size to a football pitch. They weren't very high, only about five metres tall. Every team was constructing an identical building at the same pace.

Every day, our commander would give us all specific jobs to do, expecting it to last the whole day. He was normally right, we would never finish early, but if someone was running behind schedule, we would all have to wait until they were done. Nobody wanted to be that person. My job was simply to move stuff, whether it was rock, or carrying things for other people to build with. It was hard work and fast-paced (I had to be fast, or the builders would fall behind schedule). We would get one break a day where an elder would bring us a bottle of water, a piece of fruit and a bowl of rice and chicken. The food was basic and not filling, but we never complained. After a day of work, we would go back to our rooms where we would be given a similar dinner, something equally as basic, and if we were lucky, we would get a piece of bread too. We would then sleep, wake up, and do it all again.

The first few months of building were strange. It wasn't a case of being happy or sad, or feeling bad about what had happened; it was just about surviving. The Elders were honest and ran a very tight ship with simple rules. If you stepped out of line, it resulted in being shot by the balls they carried and vaporised instantly. There was no room to negotiate.

In the first few days and weeks, we did see the occasional person try to make a run for it or try to attack an Elder, but it was pointless, it always ended in the same way. People soon grew wise to it, too scared of the consequences to cause any trouble. I can still remember the first time I saw someone try to escape on day three. They weren't in my group, but it happened on the way out of the school grounds. He was tall with dark hair; I didn't recognise him. I don't know where he thought he was running to. As soon as he started running, the commander of his class simply lifted his arm and shot him. And, just like that, he was gone. The act of shooting had been emotionless; it was almost transactional. The Elder didn't say anything, and nobody reacted, probably too scared of the same outcome if they did. The rest of that day just continued as if nothing had happened.

Despite living in a constant state of fear, Mum and I managed to keep one another from completely losing our minds. It helped that we were all in the same boat. I had even made a good friend in our class, a twenty-three-year-old called Michael. He was in pretty good shape, and since a lot of what we were carrying was too heavy for one man, we would often work together. It took us a few weeks before we started talking. He had lost everyone in the invasion – his parents, his brother and his girlfriend. He and his family had been having a party at his parents' while watching Professor Watson on TV. When an Elder had come to collect them, Michael's family had tried to run, sharing the same fate as Claire and Dad. Michael had remained sitting on his knees in the house, waiting and hoping to be killed, but had instead woken up in the school courtyard.

We only spoke of our shared tragedy once. After that, we kept our discussions focused on work, and the future.

One night, Michael and I were in the far corner of the room, all the tables and chairs removed to create space for sleeping. I had my bowl in my one hand and my spoon in the other, eating slowly to make the most of it. I was between mouthfuls and staring at my bowl when I asked Michael what he thought we were building. Michael chewed for a few seconds, then swallowed.

'I'm not too sure, mate. Probably somewhere to lock up the rest of us.'

'Really?'

'Nah, they probably won't hurt us. I'm sure we'll all live long lives and be slaves to them forever.' He looked up from his bowl and smiled sarcastically.

'Well, at least we have that to look forward to, then.'

Michael laughed. 'It's a great time to be alive, Jack, a great time.'

I nudged him with my knee. 'Don't be like that, Mike,

it could be worse.'

'How?'

I shrugged. 'I don't know. We could be given the slimy pork and rice thing again, or whatever it's meant to be.'

Michael smiled and shook his head at the poor joke. 'Yeah, you're right. That would be worse.'

I knew Michael was barely holding it together most days, so I tried my best to keep him from spiralling. It didn't help that we were living like robots; our routine was so strict and repetitive, we just did everything without thinking. It was existing rather than living. I was in no way over anything that had happened, I was just so used to the routine I couldn't imagine waking up and doing anything different.

Michael and I sat in silence after eating, trying to relax as best we could. I eventually got to my feet and grabbed both our bowls.

'Right, I'm going to go get some sleep. Tomorrow is a big day. Or is it? Who knows?'

Michael lay down. 'Yeah, who knows? See you in the morning, mate.'

I put our empty bowls in the designated basket by the door, then walked towards Mum, who sat in the opposite corner, and lay down.

'Did you enjoy dinner?' Mum asked softly. She was already lying down and dozing off.

'Yeah, delicious as ever. Goodnight, Mum,' I said, rolling over to get settled. We all had one blanket and one pillow, so it wasn't exactly comfortable, but my back was used to the hard carpet now.

I lay there thinking about tomorrow before dozing off. The Elders had told us tomorrow would be the last day of building, but I wasn't nervous or excited. I told myself nothing bad was going to happen to us, and some days I even believed it. They could have killed us in a second and built the very basic buildings a hundred times faster without us. It made no sense to kill us now. I thought they had a plan for us, but I wasn't sure what.

The next morning, the door swung open. I opened my eyes slowly, still in a haze, though I had only been dozing for the last hour. In the doorway stood a tall, grey figure.

'Fifteen minutes,' it said, then shut the door.

I lay still for a few seconds before wiping my face and yawning. I stood and let out a groan, stretching my arms out as wide as they could go. I walked over to Michael in the opposite corner.

'Morning, Mike,' I said with a groan. I cleared my throat and put my arm out to help him to his feet.

'Morning, mate,' he replied, using my arm to lift himself.

We both headed out of the classroom and to the right of the door, where neatly piled clothes had been left out for us. Every day we would be provided with clean clothes – plain black trousers with a grey jumper if the weather was cold or a grey t-shirt if not. Men and women wore the same attire. There was also a basket with underwear, towels and toiletries. We had all been provided with our own black workman boots.

I grabbed what I needed and made my way to the toilet, where there were two wash basins. I walked to the one furthest from the door and Michael stood at the other. We both turned on the taps and removed the grey t-shirt and shorts provided to sleep in. I splashed myself with water and applied shower gel before passing the bottle to Michael.

'How did you sleep?' I asked, trying to make conversation.

'As well as anyone can sleeping on a classroom floor. You?'

'Not too badly.' I dried myself and brushed my teeth, then got changed into my new clothes. On our way back to the classroom, we threw our dirty clothes into the basket outside our room before going back in. Once everyone was ready, we walked out into the courtyard and stood in a line to wait.

Other lines were now moving, and Commander Wilson stood at the front of ours with his hands behind his back, staring down our line as if he was looking directly at every one of us. The Elder gave his orders and that was that. He had no sympathy for any of us; no understanding; no respect. He saw us for what we were: weak and under his rule. He always stood at the front, unflinching, so tall and powerful you could feel his authority even at the back of the line.

The line next to ours started moving, and Commander Wilson turned away and started walking towards the gate without a word, with us silently following like dogs.

It was a fifteen-minute walk to our building. There were hundreds of buildings, all in perfect lines of twenty. Though they all looked the same, our building in the middle was easy to find as we had followed the same route every day. We all lined up outside, facing Commander Wilson, too scared to make a sound. We had finally finished the construction. What was he going to say? I wasn't sure what the date was, but the sky was blue, and I could see the sun bouncing off Commander Wilson's big eyes. He looked up and down the line, then began to speak.

'Congratulations on finishing your first task. You have successfully completed what will now be your sleeping quarters. Last night, the Elders installed beds. This is now where you will stay. On each bed you will find a name card, a timetable and a watch. This is now your life. Every four weeks, you will find a new timetable, consisting of building work, lessons and chores. Your watches are identical and set to the same time; there is no excuse for running late to any of your appointments. If you are, you will be punished.

'You will learn more over the course of the coming months, but let me make something clear: nothing has changed. If you continue to do as you are told, no harm will come to you, but if you step out of line, whether that be with each other or an Elder, it will be the end of you.

'You may now enter your dorm. An Elder will return at 1:00 p.m. with lunch.'

Commander Wilson stood for a few more seconds, looking up and down the line, then walked off. Everyone continued to stand still. Every day until now we had had Elders everywhere, watching us like hawks, but now we were alone. I looked around, trying to inherit some bravery or courage from another person, but nobody moved until the person at the end of the line opened the door to the dorm and everyone began to follow in single file.

I ought to run away; to escape with Mum. But we had nowhere to run to. We couldn't run back to our old life, after all. No, I knew deep down I was safer here, so I followed the line into our dorm.

Inside were rows of beds in four lines, and the Elders had also put LED strip lights on the roof.

A man in his mid-forties turned to me with a confused look on his face. 'They've put lights up overnight?'

He wasn't in my class, but I had been building with him for three months. I wasn't sure of his name – it might have been John – but it was too late to ask now.

I replied with an equally confused look on my face. 'I guess they don't really need us for any of this.'

'They must have left the electricity on, or maybe they're getting the power from somewhere else.'

I shrugged. I didn't know what they had done overnight or anything about power. But having seen spaceships, aliens, and people annihilated by lasers, wondering about how they managed to get the lights up and working so quickly seemed trivial. Maybe they had used a different type of power? Either way, it didn't make a difference to our situation.

Mum had already found her bed and I gave her a look to indicate that I was going to look for mine. She nodded her understanding.

I found it on the fourth row right at the back. It didn't

take too long to find it, and by the time I got there, most of the other beds were taken. Luckily, I had been placed next to Mike. He was already there, putting on his watch. I looked at his name card, then back at him.

'Looks like we're neighbours, Michael Anderson,' I said with a grin.

He looked down at my card. 'It looks like we are, Jack Palmer.'

I put on my black watch. It didn't show the date, but did have a couple of buttons on the side that I guessed were for setting alarms. I picked up my name card and timetable.

The plan for my life, and all I could ever amount to, had been reduced to a single piece of paper.

What a way to live.

15

It was kind of like being at school, the new system. We still spent a lot of time building: showers and washrooms, canteens, sport halls – any type of building that could serve a purpose. All the buildings were always very basic. Often, we would build the shell, then awake one morning to find lights and other details had been provided by the Elders. We assembled so many buildings that the sleeping quarters were now known as the Rejuvenance District.

We had a lesson every day, where we learnt either skills that would make us useful, such as building, or the science and history of the Elders' planet, never our own. They seemed to enjoy telling us how much more advanced they were than us. We learnt about the orbs that they carried, controlled by their thoughts, which was how they could so easily make the orbs do different things depending on the situation. The power would start from within then be released through the orb. It was, of course, far too advanced for us to fully understand.

Lessons took place in the Learning District, my old school at the hub of it, with new classrooms being built outwards in perfectly straight lines. Now that everyone in London had to go to school to learn, we needed to build hundreds of new classrooms to accommodate everyone. They were all square, eight metres by eight, and set five metres apart. And there was a sports hall on each corner at the edges of the district.

There was no money, but we didn't need it; everything was provided by the Elders. We would have breakfast, lunch and dinner in the Sustenance District. Clothes were provided to us weekly and left on our beds while we were out. We could wash these during the week in the washrooms we had built – small rooms with buckets of water for this purpose. Known as the Maintenance District, it was also where we showered.

Life was simple, and everything was routine.

If you had a skill considered to be useful, this was also listed on your timetable. For instance, we had doctors and nurses who worked in the New Life District, which we discovered was where all babies and children under thirteen were kept and cared for. There was no means of stopping pregnancies and births from happening, but despite what people had initially thought, the Elders didn't seem to mind this: in fact, they almost promoted it. All families with young children had swiftly been moved to the New Life District once it was built, and the Elders worked alongside trained humans to educate and raise the children who lived there. Everyone in the New Life District had their own private dorm, like ours, but scaled down to only four beds, and once a child reached the age of thirteen, they were moved back into the normal dorms, which Mike and I only found out when a new bed appeared in our dorm one evening alongside a lost-looking thirteen-year-old boy.

In terms of quality of life, it wasn't as bad as it could

have been. There were no wars, no rebellions, but also no sign of getting our old lives back. Fighting each other was considered just as bad as fighting an Elder. If you were caught fighting or stepping out of line, the outcome was a simple one: you were shot where you stood. No courts, no trials, just simple termination.

It was such a brutal system, that the more time went on, the less it happened, and the less it happened, the more the Elders trusted us. After a year, we could walk around and visit friends in other districts, so long as we stuck to our timetables. I couldn't remember the last time I'd seen someone get shot. If we did what we were told, we were safe.

I didn't like to think of it as us accepting our new life. It wasn't about that. It was simply a matter of acknowledging the need to survive. If we were ever going to have a chance of things returning to normal, we needed to build some kind of positive relationship with the Elders, or at least pretend to.

Fortunately, unlike Commander Wilson, some of them were keen to do the same. I had become quite close to the Elder teaching us Elder history, Dr Lewis. He could always be found in his room or on the school grounds, and we would often speak after class. I even started visiting him in my free time, just to learn more about the aliens who had invaded our planet.

The end of the first year of our post-invasion life also marked the introduction of a new piece of technology to the district. It was a screen, three metres tall and a metre wide, that worked as an interactive map, showing how the new order looked and where all the districts were located.

The districts could even be selected, and you could search all the names of the people who lived there. It was a few days after this was introduced that I found out that Amy and David both lived in identical towns, made up of identical districts, just a few miles away.

Life was taking shape. But one thing I had learnt over the first year of the new order was that everything could change in an instant. You never knew what was waiting just around the corner.

16

Some days, it was hard to remember how life used to be. Three years since the Elders first invaded Earth, and I'm now eighteen, 6ft, and in good shape from the years of physical activity and eating a restricted diet. I still didn't know or care what month it was, all I knew was that it was probably summer: it was a nice day, warm with clear skies.

I was currently at the front of a classroom (which I had helped to build) with Michael and Dr Lewis. We had just finished a history lesson, the last item on my timetable, so I was in no rush to head back before dinner.

'You know you get to pick your names?' I began, addressing my question to Dr Lewis.

'Yes?'

'Did you all pick your titles depending on your roles?'

He glanced over at Michael, then back at me, knowing I was up to something; we were always trying to goad a reaction.

'Yes. But it was more about picking names that humans could identify with. It wasn't a long process; it was just a matter of matching up two words. I have no emotional attachment to the name.'

'I was just wondering if anyone picked something more famous, like Dr Dre.' I knew I probably had a childish grin on my face – I may have grown older, but I still hadn't grown up. Yes, my jokes weren't the most mature or clever, but they helped get me through the day.

He looked down to the pages of work on his desk. 'No, Jack. Dr Dre was an American rapper, record producer and entrepreneur, not a doctor. We also do not copy names.'

He always responded with facts, never lowering himself to my juvenile jokes.

'You know who Dr Dre was?' Michael asked, surprised.

'I know everything about human history, Michael.'

Dr Lewis had the same arrogance as the other Elders, though I didn't think he meant anything by it; he simply spoke in facts, which came across like he thought he knew more than you. To be fair, he did.

'It doesn't matter now, anyway,' Michael said, a hint of venom in his voice. 'Music isn't a luxury we get to enjoy anymore.'

'We have choir,' I interjected, trying to calm Michael down.

The choir was a group of people who enjoyed singing and would meet weekly to sing together and perform in different canteens throughout the week. They were really very good, and the Elders didn't object as long as they exclusively sung songs they had written themselves. There were a few other social groups too, though people had to ensure the Elders approved and that any leisure activities were inoffensive.

None of this was good enough for Michael, though. He didn't seem to understand that if we wanted to live, really live, we had to *try*. Most of our conversations ended with him making a bitter jab at our new lives and walking off, and I knew this one would be no different.

'It isn't the same,' he muttered. 'I'm going back to the dorms. See you later.'

Dr Lewis nodded in farewell. 'Goodbye, Michael.'

I wasn't sure whether or not he realised Michael resented everything that had happened and had no intention of accepting this way of life. Dr Lewis was intelligent, but reading social cues wasn't his strong suit – to be honest, none of the Elders were particularly well versed in human emotions.

I leaned by elbows against the desk. 'I need some help, DL. Michael is a great guy, and over the years he's been such a help, to me and Mum, but I can't think of a way to thank him. Not that he would want, anyway.' I paused for a second. 'More than anything, I just want to find a way to help him be happier here.'

The more time went by, the more I worried about Michael. He really had been a big help to me; I'd never had a big brother, but I could imagine this was what it would be like. He was always there to lend a hand; help explain something if I didn't understand. I always knew he was there for me and had my back through it all. He wouldn't appreciate me saying it – he was only eight years older than me, after all – but at times he felt like a father to me as well. Having Michael around also helped Mum feel more confident that I was doing okay. Making sure I grew up safely in this post-invasion world was my mum's only priority.

'Michael is doing fine, Jack. He listens and doesn't put himself in danger. That is enough.'

'What do you mean by enough?' I asked, frustrated.

'How old were you, Jack, when the invasion happened?'

'Fifteen.'

'How old was Michael?'

'Twenty-three.'

Dr Lewis nodded. 'You were young, you were at school, and your life was still taking shape. Michael had his life, he had his job, his partner, his family, and a sense of direction. He thought he knew where his life was going, then in a matter of minutes, that was taken from him. Not everyone can recover from that. The New Life Districts are full of people your age and younger, people who have made lives here for themselves. They are happy because they have a family, their lives unknown until now. But Michael knew where his life was going and has no intention of trying to make a new life for himself here. You just have to accept that.'

'But I don't accept it! I lost my life too! My dad, my little sister, my best friends. What about my mum? She's older than Michael, but she's doing okay. But if she wasn't, I wouldn't have given up on her, and I won't give up on him either.'

I had so many thoughts going through my head. We rarely talked about the invasion, but when we did, old emotions always resurfaced. It was strange talking about it with Dr Lewis – in some ways it always felt like he sympathised with humans. It was easy to forget we were on different sides.

'That's different,' he replied, not acknowledging my emotional reaction.

'How? How is it different?'

'She had you. She *had* to be strong. And as long as she still has you, still has a purpose, she will continue to make the best of her situation *You* were young and have come to accept this way of life; you know that thinking constantly about the past will not bring your sister or father back. Time heals all wounds eventually. Michael is simply healing more slowly.'

'It isn't about *accepting* our new lives though, is it? If I don't obey, I die. I don't have a choice.' I didn't want him thinking I was happy here. I was simply making the best of a bad situation.

'Correct, and you have learned to live with that. Everyone is different. Michael could easily have been one of the people who tried to escape or who attacked someone. Be grateful he is still here and doing as well as he is.' Dr Lewis looked down at his papers.

Conversation over, I guess.

It didn't escape me what Dr Lewis was really trying to say: Michael could have been killed a long time ago. I had to be grateful he was still here.

As I walked back to the dorm, I thought about everything we had spoken about. I didn't often let myself dwell on the past; he was right about that. I had become an adult here, and although I vividly remembered life before the invasion, I didn't know what the future or *my* future would look like. Maybe age was a big part of it. There were people now with families who were genuinely happy and satisfied with their lives. I often thought about Dad and Claire, but I knew they weren't coming back, and I had tried to move on.

Michael didn't want to move on. But he was still here, so he must still want to live, or feel like he had a purpose. I just needed to be patient with him and be glad I still had him around.

I just hoped he wouldn't let his anger drive him to do something that could get him hurt… or worse.

17

I'd decided to eat by myself that evening, as I was planning on meeting Amy and David later, so I needed to eat quickly. Humans were allowed to leave their district and visit others, but it was policed and only permissible under strict conditions. If these conditions were broken, a district could be placed into lockdown for any amount of time, ranging from a couple of days to months.

In order to leave, we had to get our arm stamped by our district supervisor – an Elder, though fortunately we had been freed from the clutches of Commander Wilson – with the letters PTR (Permission to Roam). Then we had to register our entrance with the district supervisor of the place we were visiting. Finally, we had to be back by midnight, and not a minute later.

The rules were simple but effective: if we were seen out of our districts either without a stamp or out of hours, we were considered to be 'attempting to escape' and would be killed on the spot. It was almost hilarious, in a darkly funny way. Why would anyone try to escape when there was nowhere to escape to? The districts were all, for the most part, the same. No one was experiencing a better life than anyone else.

Entering the canteen, I walked up to the service counter and greeted the men and women behind it. They changed so regularly that I rarely had a chance to get to know any of them. It was like a typical school dinner production line, with everyone doing a specific job. Whether it was serving the vegetables or the main dish, they were always organised and efficient, and the queue moved quickly.

Fortunately, the meals had improved significantly over the years, though some days I did crave pizza and chips. The Elders were very strict about what we put into our bodies: they wanted us to be healthy and always ensured our food was nutritious. Carrying my tray over to one of the five long tables, I sat and ate quickly, before taking my plate to the drop-off point by the door, which was simply a large, black container.

I then made my way to the small building opposite, where we kept the lanterns. We no longer had streetlights: like the rest of the human inventions, these were destroyed. Electricity through the main grid, how we knew it pre-invasion, had ceased to exist. These lanterns were now the only way for us to see at night-time: battery powered light sources, with a handle on the top, that let out light from all angles.

It was summertime, before sundown – 6:02 p.m. to be precise – and the sky was still blue. Yet I knew it would be dark by the time I got back from visiting my two oldest friends, so I was organised and collected a lantern for the way back. I wished I had been as organised earlier – shorts and a t-shirt were perfect for now, but I knew by nightfall I would regret my decision not to pick up a jumper.

Sighing, I began the walk to David's district, swinging the lantern in my right hand. Despite my intense conversation with Dr Lewis and Mike earlier in the day, the weather had kept me in a good mood. Over the last few years, I had made this walk hundreds of times – we tried to meet as often as we could – and though it was not a particularly scenic route, it would be a peaceful journey as it was always quiet. The further out of town I went, the more buildings were replaced by trees, nature reclaiming the land. When the Elders destroyed our world three years ago, they were mindful of Earth's green spaces and seemed to appreciate its natural elements. The odd watch building could be seen amid the greenery, erected for security purposes to ensure no trouble occurred outside the towns. Taller and narrower than all the others we'd built, with stairs that spiralled all the way to a platform at the top, the watch buildings were manned by whichever four people were on duty that day, one on each side, gazing into the distance on the off chance of trouble. Like every other duty, security was included on our timetables. It was one of my least favourite tasks – it was a tedious job. Sometimes, I would hope for trouble just to keep myself from dozing off, but it never came (everyone was too well-behaved). Occasionally, an Elder would join us, to check we were doing our job, but these days most of us were trusted to do as we were told.

Where I lived, there wasn't much wildlife, and there were barely any trees, so the walk to David's district always felt like an adventure. There were no man-made paths anymore, just natural passages that had formed where everyone took the same route when visiting local districts. It was always fairly quiet walking from town to town, but as it was a nice day, I expected to see at least a few people during the thirty-minute walk; a few Elders too. We walked the same routes, and if we were behaving, they would mind their own business and we would ours. If it was an Elder I knew, sometimes they would even acknowledge me and say hello. We didn't socialise with them (we knew where we stood in this new society), but they were fair; they weren't cruel unless we stepped out of line.

I still vividly remember the day I first found my friends, the day the map of all the different districts was set up for us. My heart was pounding as I frantically poked at different districts, desperately searching both their names. I'm not sure how I would have reacted if I hadn't found them, but I consider myself extremely lucky that I did.

Once I knew where David and Amy lived, getting in touch turned out to be straightforward: I simply got my PTR pass signed in both Amy and David's towns, then started asking people if they knew them. Getting back in touch with them was without a doubt the biggest game changer post-invasion. Seeing them both again gave me hope; something different to look forward to. It gave me people to have a laugh with; to talk to about life before the invasion.

We *had* changed as people though – unsurprising really, given how much had happened over the last three years. Amy's family had all survived the invasion, and she had confided in me that, some days, the guilt that they had all made it when so many other families had suffered ate her up inside. She was immensely grateful for her family, and remained close to her parents and older sister Rebecca, who now lived in the New Life District with her partner,

James, and son, Robert.

When David had told me that both his parents had been killed, it was like someone had punched me in the stomach. I'd had Mum to help me survive in the early days; it was devastating to think that Dave had been forced to get through it all alone. It made me angry, yet also incredibly proud of him, when I thought of the strength and courage he must have shown to survive alone at only fifteen.

Thankfully, Dave had maintained his spirit, despite it all, and though things were different between us, we had managed to find our way back to bantering about stupid things we'd done and discussing meaningless trivia. Dave had lost so much, but deep down, he'd never lost who he was.

Unlike me, Dave had quickly found himself a partner, Jessica, and they now lived in the New Life District of their town with their son, Joshua. As had been the case for many people, they had decided to try for a baby within a few months of being together, in the hope they could get a home to themselves in the New Life District. It had worked, but unlike for many people, they were still happy, and very much in love. It was weird seeing Dave interact with Jessica and Joshua – I'd only known him as an irresponsible teen, but now, he was not only a supportive partner, but a loving father too. My life had changed a lot, sure, but I still felt like a kid in many ways. Dave was a proper adult, with people he was responsible for. It was weird to think about.

As I arrived at David's home in the New Life District, I found him sitting outside with Jessica and Amy in the sunshine. David looked up and smiled, his grin still as cheesy as ever. His hair was still blond and messy, but now he had a beard to match, and his build was thickset, like a heavy weight boxer. You would be forgiven for finding him intimidating. As soon as he smiled though, his friendly face and a warm presence quickly put people at ease.

'Jack! Get over here, asshole.'

'And a good evening to you too. Where's Josh?'

'On a playdate,' Jessica answered with a proud smile. 'He'll be dropped off soon though.'

'Sounds fun. How is everyone?' I asked. Everyone looked at each other, nodding in silent agreement that life was good. But Dave couldn't resist a comment.

'You know, Jack, I actually hurt my elbow this morning building a new watchtower. Think I might have pulled something.' He moaned, a grimace on his face, and rubbed his elbow, pointing it at me as though I couldn't possibly know what an elbow was.

I gently patted him on the shoulder as a gesture of sympathy. 'For a big man, you're always injured. Guess you're not as young as you used to be.'

'Don't you remember, Jack? He was always getting injured when he was young as well,' Amy interjected.

David held his hand to his chest dramatically, as if someone had deeply insulted him. 'I was *never* injured!'

'Yeah, he just enjoyed a moan,' I said, leaning back on my elbows. 'Unfortunately for us, he was fit every week to play football.'

Jessica cackled. 'He still loves a moan, definitely no change there.'

We usually tried to keep out conversations light-hearted

and rarely spoke about anything too deep and meaningful. If something had happened worth talking about, then we could be serious, but on the whole we met up as a distraction from what was going on around us. When Joshua was dropped off, he provided much-needed entertainment, toddling about and babbling good-naturedly before he was carried off for a bath and then bed.

There wasn't much to do except chat, so we tended to spend our meetings trying to entertain each other and playing games. We had made a deck of cards to pass the time. David considered himself an expert poker player, but he couldn't hide a good hand. Eventually, it was too dark to play, so we continued chatting for an hour before saying our goodbyes. We were meeting again in five days, so we wouldn't be apart for long.

Amy and I turned on our lanterns and began our journeys home – we could walk together for the first ten minutes before we had to go our separate ways. It was a clear night with stars covering the sky. I supposed one good thing that came from the invasion was no more light pollution. Now that we knew aliens existed, we knew there was an expansive array of life out there, and that only made me more fascinated. Each star was its own mystery. They shone brighter than they ever had before, the sky pitch-black and covered in bright, beautiful dots, each one a beacon of hope that there was something else out there; something better.

'I wish I had my jumper,' I grumbled, teeth chattering.

'Dumb decision. Doesn't your mum lay your clothes out for you anymore?' Amy said with a smirk.

'Hilarious. I'm lucky grey is my colour.' We paused for a second before I moved the conversation on to keep my mind off the cold. 'Talking of parents, aren't Dave and Jessica doing an amazing job? I never thought I'd see the day when Dave took something seriously.'

'Yeah, they seem really happy, all things considered.'

'Have you ever thought about children?'

'No,' Amy replied without a second's thought.

'Why? You could get your own house, and there's no crime or war or poverty anymore – in a messed up way, the world is safer now than it ever has been.'

Amy sighed. 'But they wouldn't be free, Jack.' She paused to gather her thoughts. 'We know this is our life now and we have all come to accept that. It hasn't been easy, but we haven't had a choice. We all go about our days acting as if everything is normal and fine, but it isn't. I know exactly how kids today will grow up, how their lives will pan out. I know how everyone's will. We live by timetables and do what we are told in order to survive. We don't get to choose what we do; we don't get to choose anything, not even what we have for dinner. That isn't a life for a child; it isn't a life for anyone, and I don't want to bring someone else into this world when I know that's what their life will be like.'

I wrapped my arm around her shoulders, pulling her into my side. 'Sorry, Amy, I didn't mean to upset you. I know it's a horrible situation, and I agree with you. I get why people are having kids, and I don't blame them, but you're right.' I stared up at the sky. 'You know, I often wonder what it all means. Why not just kill us all? Why keep us living this way? What's their endgame? Do they even have one?'

Amy shrugged, resting her head against my shoulder. 'I'm not sure. Maybe.' She paused again. 'Whatever happens, I don't think freedom is going to be an option.'

I felt my jaw clench, the anger I tried to keep pushed down rising to the surface. 'You're right. This isn't really living, is it?'

Amy looked up to the stars, as if searching for an answer. 'No. But it isn't even that. I'm not saying I would have become something amazing before, but at least it would have been my decision what to do with my life; my future. Now, everything is decided for us. We're prisoners, Jack. We have to keep reminding ourselves of that.'

'Luckily, Michael won't let me forget it. And, for what it's worth, I'm certain you would have done something amazing with your life.'

We had arrived at the point in the journey where we went our separate ways, so I gave her a quick hug and we reluctantly said goodnight. I didn't really want to leave her in the mood she was in, but if we lingered too long, we'd miss curfew, or get spotted by one of the watchers and reprimanded.

It was strange. I could go months without thinking about the situation we were in. But when I did, it was like an itch that couldn't be scratched, and old repressed emotions would come flooding back to the surface. There were people like Amy, who obviously thought about it more than I did; there were people like Michael, who seemed to think about it every day and night. I usually

tried to remain positive, but tonight, I thought about it all
the way home.

18

6:30 a.m. and my watch started beeping. It was a high-pitched beep, each one short, sharp, and piercing. The sound would always ring painfully in my ears. A lot had changed over the years, but my dread of mornings had not. I rolled onto my back, pressing the top button on my watch to stop the alarm. We had a window in the middle of every wall, but I was in the corner, so didn't get much natural light to wake me up.

I blinked the sleep out my eyes and yawned, sluggishly turning over, both feet hitting the floor like two lead blocks. I leaned forward, stretching my back with my arms up. Despite still being young, years of heavy lifting had taken its toll, most noticeably in the morning, the aches and pains becoming gradually worse with each passing year. I looked to find Michael had already gone. He wasn't a good sleeper, and was always up before me. During the night, I would often hear his short, heavy breaths as he fought against the nightmares that still plagued him. I was lucky in that department. My mind seemed to have repressed most of my worst memories.

At the canteen, I joined the queue for breakfast: scrambled egg and mushroom with a glass of orange juice. I sat with Mum and her friend, Julie, who were both up before me. Julie and Mum were of a similar age and had both lost a lot during the invasion, so they took solace in the fact that they could help each other through the tough times.

'Morning,' I said gruffly, not yet fully awake.

'Morning, Jack, what have you got on today?' Julie asked.

The years of unhappiness were etched in every deep line on her face, her features pointy and sharp. Yet Julie was much more affectionate than her appearance suggested, and over the years, she had been like a second parent to me. I was lucky to have a number of people still looking out for me who I could turn to.

'I've got a lot of building,' I replied. 'What about you two?'

'We're nursing for most of the day, then have a lesson later this afternoon.'

The Medical District was a ten-minute walk away and the buildings were identical to the dorms. Inside were rows of beds, where the patients would stay while recovering, though it didn't look like a hospital and had no medical equipment. The Elders were the doctors, healing with their advanced technology, like the orbs. Recovery time was quick, never more than a few days. Everything the Elders did was based around efficiency, and that included health. All cancers had been eradicated, and as a race, humans had never been so fit and well. There were very few things they couldn't cure, and there were only two ways off this planet for humans now: elimination, or death from old age.

Due to the advanced health care, people were expected to work all the way to the end. Unfortunately, there wasn't a "Luxurious Retirement District" and everyone was expected to be a contributing member of society. If you couldn't do the heavy lifting, there were plenty of other ways to make yourself useful, and if you couldn't do those jobs? Well, you got blasted.

Nurses were placed in the Medical District to aid the Elders, mainly by helping with feeding and cleaning. If basic first aid was ever needed, the Elders usually passed that on too, usually to someone who had once been a doctor (light work for these overqualified humans). However, if it was something more serious, it was a job for the Elders, and they worked alone. In their eyes, humans were too simple-minded to help with anything that involved complex thought. Our medical science and equipment was prehistoric compared to what they had.

I looked over at Mum. 'You two are spending a lot of time over there these days. Do you think they'll get you doing some actual medical work soon?'

Though the lines on Mum's face weren't as deep as Julie's, each one told a story, mostly of loss and a hard life. Yet somehow, she still always had a smile on her face and appeared optimistic. Resilience had always been one of Mum's superpowers.

'We aren't very useful anywhere else, Jack. Best to leave the building to strong young men like you.'

'But you get air conditioning! How is that fair?'

'You get to be outdoors, Jack. Enjoy it!'

'She's right.' Julie winked at Mum. 'And that's no way to speak to your mother.'

Mum tutted, wagging her finger at me. 'He has no

respect, I tell you. None!'

Mum and Julie liked to gang up on me, always backing each other up, but it made them laugh so I never minded.

Rolling my eyes at their antics, I finished my eggs before making my way to the meeting point for building, not far from the canteen. The Elders had erected a line of twenty tall poles, a bit like lampposts, each a different colour, which corresponded to the coloured dots on our timetable. Today, my dot was red, so I went to stand by the red pole.

I only just managed to hold back my groan. Commander Wilson was our supervising Elder for the day. Great. Just what I needed. My conversation with Amy yesterday hadn't exactly improved my feelings towards the Elders, and Commander Wilson was the worst of them.

Fortunately, Michael was in my building group, and was already there and signed in. I nodded to him and he nodded back, looking as miserable as I felt. We hadn't even started our five hours of building yet. Unlike me, Michael never tried to hide his feelings or put on a brave face; in fact, at times, I was sure he just adopted a moody, unapproachable look to avoid speaking to others. He could be confrontational, but rarely held eye contact for long, keeping his glances short and intimidating. His expression never put me off, though – I knew he was a good guy underneath it all.

As I went to approach him, I was ambushed by Joe, a boy who had joined our building crew last year. He was younger than me, but Michael and I had formed a close bond with him, taking him under our wing. He was a chatterbox, full of zest, and his eagerness and spirit would often grate on Michael, but he would never say anything other than the occasional sly dig. I wouldn't say I found Joe's excitement infectious, but I did respect him for always remaining positive, and got a laugh out of how much his constant chatter and questions annoyed Michael.

'Michael doesn't seem in a good mood, does he?' Joe remarked.

'I've not spoken with him yet, but is he ever?'

I'd never understood how someone could have as much oomph in the morning as Joe did. He reminded me of Laura in so many ways, and the thought always sent a jolt of sadness through my chest.

'But he seems particularly grumpy, don't you think?' Joe pressed, as if he thought I knew something he didn't.

'Let's go and find out.'

We began walking over to Michael, and the look he gave us made me think that making conversation was going to be a bigger chore than the building work, especially since Joe had a knack for gradually exhausting Michael throughout the day.

Luckily for Michael, at that moment, Commander Wilson called us all to attention, and we headed off.

We began our walk in our usual single file behind the commander, like a well-oiled machine. We were building a new watch tower, twenty minutes outside of town. Upon arrival, we all got into our positions, which we had previously been assigned when starting the job. Michael, Joe and I all had the same job of moving and positioning the materials correctly, mainly heavy lifting.

The tower was currently two metres high, so we still had

over eight metres to go. We had ladders and scaffolding made from wood to assist with building, but everything else was old-fashioned manpower, not a machine in sight. The stones would be cut on the floor to become brick-like, though much larger than standard house bricks, and it was then our job to carry them to the bricklayers. Constructing a watch tower meant passing bricks up to each of the layers, which was hard, physical labour.

The sun blazing down from the cloudless sky didn't help our efforts. The ground sent up a disorienting haze and the grass stood still, as if it was too hot to move. I could almost see the heat bouncing off Joe's sunburned face as the energy he'd had this morning began to wane. Perspiration was pouring out of me, never ending. I stood up straight and wiped the beads of sweat from my forehead. I looked up at Michael, who was passing up another brick, and could see his muscles straining and the sun reflecting off the sweat on his arms. It wasn't long until lunch, and I could sense people getting hot and frustrated.

'Put your back into it, Mike!' I shouted playfully.

'Yeah, come on, Mikey! You're slowing us all down,' Joe added in his high-pitched voice. He was always able to find energy from somewhere to wind Michael up.

Michael was red, though I wasn't sure if it was rage or the sun, but either way he was glowing, steam practically coming out of his ears like an old-fashioned cartoon.

'I swear that when this tower is done, I'm going to throw you both off it.'

'Irrelevant, Mikey, I'm indestructible,' Joe answered, looking to me for approval and adding a cheeky wink.

The difference between me and Joe was that I knew it was always best to quit while I was ahead.

'Let's put that to the test, shall we?' Michael snarled as he marched towards Joe.

Before Michael had even taken his first step, Joe had dived behind me for cover. It wasn't a wise decision, as I had no intention of helping him and wouldn't be able to stop Michael even if I wanted to. Michael was, of course, only messing around, even if he did want to throttle Joe. This was just Joe and Michael's relationship; they were like a cat and dog, always bickering.

I had seen the same routine hundreds of times before and I would see it a hundred more. This was just a typical day for me. It wasn't glamorous or dangerous, it was just ordinary. Every day was unexceptional, every day the same; and I had become accustomed to that.

The problem was, if drama was to come, bad news usually came with it.

19

A few weeks passed routinely, and we were back at the watchtower approaching the final leg of the project. It was now just over six metres tall and wrapped in wooden scaffold beams. The beams were heavy logs tied together in squares that we used to climb up the tower. Michael was standing halfway up on a beam, while Joe and I passed bricks up to him that he then passed to the bricklayer at the top.

It was a simple task, made difficult by the weather. We'd had a few weeks of sun and blue skies, but last night there had been a thunderstorm. The winds had picked up and clouds rolled in. The storm lasted the duration of the night. Lightning had lit up the whole dorm, followed by thunder echoing loudly. With so much rain falling, it had drummed against the roof, making a continuous pattering noise. This had made it difficult to sleep, so everyone was tired and lacking concentration on a day when it needed to be heightened. All night I had just hoped it would stop by the morning.

It had not.

The thunder and lightning had died down, but the rain continued furiously with no signs of slowing down; the flood gates of the sky had opened. The rain was incessant, snapping and crackling like a bushfire. The sky was still ominous, the clouds unmoving and threatening. It was still the summer and humid, the rain leaving a zesty smell in the nostrils. You could be forgiven for believing we were in some tropical climate, not a suburb of London. Puddles had formed all around us and there was a pitter-patter sound as the rain bounced off the stones. Droplets of moisture dripped from the leaves of the surrounding trees, and visibility was drastically reduced. Both our sight and hearing had been severely compromised.

The main problem was that everything had become slippery, making an already difficult job even more so. Joe was passing a stone up to Michael and I could tell by Joe's body language and expression that he was nervous, although he always tried to act as if nothing bothered him.

'It's all right, Joe, I've got it,' Michael reassured him. He was crouched on a beam and took the stone before standing and placing it above his head on the wall. The beams were a foot wide and flat to stand on, but there was not a lot of room to manoeuvre.

'I know its fine, Michael.'

I think Joe was trying to convince himself as much as us that he wasn't nervous.

When it was my turn to pass Michael a stone, I quickly realised I didn't have a good grip, and I could feel it slipping between my fingers, the harshness of the stone and relentless rain making my hands red and inflamed. I adjusted my grip, but it didn't help much.

As I looked up at Michael, rain was filling my eyes, my vision blurred. 'Are you ready?'

'Yep. Not long now, Jack,' Michael replied, reaching for

the stone and lifting it with ease.

Relieved, I climbed down and went to collect another stone. I was soaked and miserable, my t-shirt and trousers sticking to me. All I could think about was a warm shower and food, when I looked over to watch Joe pass his stone up to Michael. The beam had become smooth and wet from the moisture and, as Michael stood, he suddenly lost his footing.

I stared in horror as Michael fell heavily to the ground. First the stone hit the floor with a loud crack and thud before Michael landed next to it, just as loudly. I was paralyzed by fear as I stood looking at him. Michael wasn't moving.

I held my breath, watching.

Then, slowly, he moved, rolling over onto his side. He was winded and struggling to catch his breath. I started running over to him, but paused as Commander Wilson walked over. He towered over Michael with an intimidating dominance, like an animal staking a territorial claim. He looked down at Michael with his big, black, bug-like eyes. They seemed soulless, and looking into them was like looking into a black hole.

'Get up,' he said in his eerie robotic tone.

Commander Wilson did not know any of our names; he only ever gave us orders. As far as he was concerned, we were just objects for him to order and rule.

The rain was bouncing off him, his smooth grey skin gleaming. The shine it gave him accentuated the definition of his muscles on his slim build. While everyone else was struggling in the conditions, Commander Wilson looked to be in his element.

Michael groaned and spat blood onto the floor. He was staring blankly into his reflection in the puddle he had just landed in, as if mentally preparing himself for what he was about to do. Them, he looked up at Commander Wilson.

There was no fear in his eyes. Only rage.

I felt all my muscles seize up as terror gripped me. *Please, don't do anything stupid.*

'Give me a second. I landed on my back.'

I had never seen anyone speak to Commander Wilson so directly.

'I said get up,' Commander Wilson snarled.

'And I said give me a second.'

There was no possible outcome where Michael could win this battle. They stared at each other for a couple of seconds, neither of them flinching or blinking. I could see the muscles in Commander Wilson's arms clench and move as he gripped his orb tighter.

Elders didn't ask for a third time.

I realised the severity of the situation and shook myself out of my paralysed state. Panic washed over me, but I knew I had to do something. I ran over and dragged Michael up from the ground with all my strength. Michael stood for a second, looking up at Commander Wilson, neither of them breaking eye contact. They seemed to be staring through each other's faces and into their souls.

I yanked Michael away towards the stones. There was to be no epic fight today.

Commander Wilson stood for a few more seconds just watching Michael. Everyone knew that, if he wanted to, he could kill Michael, and Commander Wilson wanted to make sure everyone took note of that fact before moving on.

'What were you thinking?' I hissed as we hobbled away. 'Are you trying to get yourself killed?'

'So what if I am? This isn't living. I'm done with it.' Michael was looking past me, as if to see whether Commander Wilson was still there.

'What do you mean you're done?'

'I mean I'm done, Jack. I'm not doing this anymore.' He walked past me before I had a chance to ask any more questions. He brushed past Joe too (who had been rooted to the spot throughout the whole ordeal) and climbed back up onto the beam upon which he had previously been standing.

We continued the rest of the morning without saying another word to each other. His last words echoed round my brain.

I'm done.

20

The rest of the day passed awkwardly. I kept looking over at Michael, who may have physically been there, but mentally he was clearly somewhere else. He wouldn't look at me or talk to me, but I could tell what had happened that morning was still bothering him. He looked like a volcano about to erupt. I wanted to speak to him to make sure he was alright (and that he wasn't going to do something stupid) but needed to find the right time. He had always been there for me, but now I felt I needed to be there for him. Yet I didn't really know how to play that role or how best to approach the situation; I didn't want to antagonise him or bring unwanted attention to the matter. The uncertainty got to me and I could feel anxiety curling in my stomach. Michael was avoiding me; likely he knew I was going to try to calm him down or talk him out of whatever decision he had just come to.

Panicked and determined to find a solution, I decided to seek advice from Dr Lewis.

Despite being an Elder, I had never felt threatened by Dr Lewis. He was like a counsellor to me, and always gave helpful, objective advice. I always felt like he cared, which was an uncommon trait amongst Elders. His voice and face may have been identical to the rest of them, but he always wanted to listen and help where he could.

When I explained what had happened earlier that morning, he was shocked that Michael wasn't made an example of. Apparently, even amongst the Elders, Commander Wilson always wanted to show his stature, power and dominance and wouldn't normally be that merciful. Dr Lewis recommended staying away from Commander Wilson, and suggested Michael do the same.

'Commander Wilson won't stand for anything from Michael now and will have his card marked, he will be looking for any excuse…'

He didn't have to finish the thought. I knew what he meant. If Michael stepped out of line again, Commander Wilson would kill him.

The clouds were beginning to break and the sky was tinted with blue. I hoped the change in weather may also change the current mood. I wouldn't describe it as a nice evening, but it was calm. The improving weather had certainly helped cheer me up. I just wished it would do the same for Michael.

I had dinner with Mum as usual, though I didn't eat much; the stress of the day had affected my appetite. Mum noticed, of course, and asked if anything was wrong, but I just brushed her off, blaming exhaustion. I didn't want to tell her what had happened with Michael. She was fond of him; over the years he had become like a second son to her. He didn't need looking after, but she still loved and cared for him, like a mother would her son. I didn't want to worry her. Plus, she would have been furious that I had interfered and potentially put myself in danger.

After dinner, we headed back to our dorm, and I went

straight over to my bed. Michael wasn't back yet. It was still early, so I thought little of it, falling onto my bed and laying on my back, looking up at the ceiling. It felt good to be off my feet and I felt silly for spending the whole day in a semi-state of fear. I thought about what to say to Michael, but the more I thought about it, the more I wanted to avoid saying anything to him at all. My eyes became heavy so I let myself give in to the exhaustion.

Tomorrow was a new day.

21

I woke up to the sound of my alarm ringing in my ears. I wished for five more minutes of sleep. I had slept the whole night, but still wanted longer, the physical and mental exhaustion from the day before still lingering. I sat up in my usual sluggish manner, facing Michael's bed. He wasn't there, but that wasn't unusual. He must have got up and left the dorm already. As an early riser, in the old world he would have been the model employee. I would be with him all day, so would speak to him then (or not at all, depending on his mood).

I went through my usual morning routine automatically, The air felt fresh as I stepped outside, and it was a comfortable temperature. At least building wouldn't be so miserable today. The blue sky was dotted with a few white clouds, but they looked like they weren't going to cause any harm.

I walked over to the red pole, our meeting point, and signed myself in. There were only a few minutes until we would begin our walk and continue building. Joe was standing there with his chest puffed out like a peacock, and I knew he was likely about to say something cocky and irritating.

'Fancy a lie-in did you, Jack?'

For once, he'd arrived before me.

'We still have five minutes until we have to start.'

'I know, but I can't remember the last time I beat you and Michael here.'

I looked around in confusion, my eyes darting furiously from one face to the next. I had assumed Michael was somewhere else in the line.

'What do you mean? Is Michael not here yet?'

'Well can you *see* him anywhere?' Joe said jokingly, before he noticed the fear in my expression. His tone switched instantly to one of concern. 'Have you not seen him this morning?'

I shook my head, perplexed.

'Well, did he say anything to you last night?'

'I didn't see him last night either.'

'What do you mean, you didn't see him?' his gaze darted around so rapidly I thought his head might go the full way around.

'I mean I haven't seen him, Joe.' It was unfair of me really, to snap at him, but I was starting to panic.

Joe stood, still and stunned. For a second, I thought he was going to cry. I hadn't seen him like this before, and it only made my anxiety worse.

'Well, he needs to be here in the next minute or—'

It was like Commander Wilson was listening to our conversation.

'It's time, let's go!'

Not arriving on time to your duties was a serious offence. And there was a chilling glint in Commander Wilson's eyes that told me he knew Michael wasn't there, and he was very much looking forward to dealing with him.

Everyone started to move away, but Joe and I found ourselves rooted to the spot in terror, completely frozen.

Joe whispered, 'Now what?'

I didn't have an answer.

22

It was a surreal feeling, walking to the site without Michael. We shouldn't be doing this without knowing where he was, but we had no other choice. We were like lost sheep, not knowing what to do and following blindly; every step seemed like one in the wrong direction. I was still looking around as if there was an answer out there, a clue that would help make everything okay. I felt like I was having an out-of-body experience; I was looking down at myself and Joe walking like puppets on strings, not in control of our movements, carrying on as if everything was normal when all I wanted to do was cut the strings and run in the opposite direction.

Until now, we had been living in a bubble, getting by, keeping our heads down. But as we had found out all those years ago: bubbles are easy to burst.

Joe turned around and looked at me, fear etched on his face. 'What do we do, Jack? What *can* we do?'

'We have to go to work, or we'll be killed.'

It was a horrible feeling, knowing our friend was potentially in grave danger. What was harder was knowing there was nothing we could do.

'Why has Michael done this?' Joe was still asking questions of me like I was some kind of oracle, but all he was doing was mixing all the thoughts in my head.

'I'm not sure, I haven't spoken to him since after building yesterday. But we'll find out somehow. For now, just keep your head down and do your work as normal.'

I wasn't sure how we would find out where Michael was, but I knew what Commander Wilson was like, and I still had Dr Lewis's words of warning fresh in my mind.

'I'm really worried, Jack. What if he's dead?' Joe's voice trembled.

'I'm worried too, but we shouldn't jump to any conclusions.' I tried to calm Joe; speculation wasn't helpful, though I was also having the same dark thoughts.

We arrived at the building site and the whole session went by in what seemed to be slow motion, seconds feeling like minutes, minutes like hours and every moment an eternity. It was impossible to focus on building without Michael. I wanted to try to find answers, but that desperation was only making me more aware of how slowly time passed. I was acutely aware of my surroundings; my senses had never been more switched on. I felt like I could hear the soil moving underneath my boots, could see every specific detail in Joe's face as if I was seeing him for the first time, could feel every single edge and crease on the stones I was carrying.

This clarity and concentration in every moment was only making time go slower. I felt like I was in shock. The work was physically demanding but my head was so preoccupied I didn't have the mental capacity to find it tiring. We had all lost people in the invasion, we had all experienced trauma, and it meant we were all very finely tuned to possible danger. There was still a hole in my life from losing my dad and Claire. I couldn't imagine losing Michael too, the man who had been like a father to me all this time.

Commander Wilson eyed our every movement as if we had done something wrong, which only added to my anxiety. I'm not sure he moved once. His eyes burned a hole in my back; it made me feel like I couldn't breathe.

After building, we walked back to the canteen, not because we were hungry but out of habit, and because we didn't know what else to do. Michael was still nowhere to be seen. We sat staring at our food when Joe finally spoke.

'Where is he, Jack?'

Until today, I had never had a serious conversation with Joe; I hadn't known he was capable of one.

I sighed, dejected. 'Let's just get through the day.'

We fell silent for the remainder of our meal before heading to our afternoon physical activity lesson, which was in the Learning District. Ours was in one of the sports halls we had built. There were new sports halls on every corner of the Learning District, as well as the central one in the old school. We would meet at the eastern hall, which was in the heart of the district with the rest of the old school grounds. There was also a large, flat patch of land next to each hall which was well-kept. We would use this when the weather was nice (or if the Elders wanted to "build character" in the rain). Today, the weather was pleasant, so I knew we would be outdoors.

We stood outside the hall waiting to meet our professor. Joe and I were silent, too stunned and confused to talk. Although physically we had to be there and carry on as normal, mentally we couldn't be further away.

It was a boy called Billy who was the first to try and get information from us regarding Michael's whereabouts. We didn't build with Billy, but he was in most of our lessons. I didn't particularly like him. He was a shady character and seemed to be a loner. I never saw him smile or "chat" with people. He never cared about what people had to say or wanted to get to know them, he just wanted information. He was always asking weird questions, as if there was a big conspiracy going on that he didn't know about. He would get what he wanted out of a conversation, then leave. I suspected he would have been the same even if Earth had not been invaded. Now, he crept over to us in his usual awkward manner with long strides, arms locked to his sides. Billy was tall and thin like a pole, his face narrow with angular cheekbones and a pointed chin, and he had small dark eyes set close together above a long, hooked nose. I always thought he shared many similarities with the Elders in appearance.

'So, where's Anderson?' Billy's voice was unsympathetic. He was always straight to the point, as if he had collected his words in his hand and thrown them at us.

'We aren't sure, Billy,' I said dismissively.

I could see Joe's head flicking between me and Billy, clearly agitated.

Billy let out a harsh laugh before continuing. 'Do you expect me to believe that, Palmer? Michael spends more time with you than anyone. You know what he's up to.'

I didn't know what to say. Luckily, Joe stepped forward, his fists clenched, his lips locked together, breathing through his nose like a raging bull.

'What's it to you, Billy?' Joe said slowly and deliberately, trying to intimidate him.

'Hey, I just want to know where he is in case he's planning something stupid that'll put the rest of us in danger or get us into another lockdown. I've heard stories of people attacking Elders and it always ends the same way. I'm not worried about Anderson, I just don't want to be caught in the crossfire.'

Joe looked at me, as if asking for permission to hit him. I shook my head.

Joe clenched his fists, but nodded at me, turning away. 'Get lost, Billy. You're always trying to worm your way into everything; this isn't all about you. Michael would never put anyone in danger, so you don't have to worry. But if I hear you making statements like that again, *I'll* put *you* in danger.'

Billy shrugged. 'If you say so. I'll be keeping a close eye on things though. Michael has a temper. If he's tried to run off, he's probably dead already.'

I had to pull Joe back to stop him pouncing on Billy; I had never seen him so angry.

'Calm down, don't get yourself in trouble,' I told him, trying to remain calm and rational.

'I hate Billy! Why is he always sticking his beak in?' Joe was still red with anger, shuffling on the spot like a boxer waiting for the bell.

He needed to settle down before our Elder arrived. News travelled fast in this mundane world and I knew it wouldn't be long until people began gossiping, I had to remain calm and not get myself dragged into any altercations.

'Do you think everyone has noticed Michael has gone?'

'Probably. We might not talk to everyone in class, but we know all their faces and names and would realise if someone was missing.'

Joe hung his head. 'This is bad, isn't it?'

I nodded, just as our Elder, Professor Jacobs, walked out of the sports hall. He looked identical to every other Elder except for a yellow armband that read PJ. He wasn't as bad as Commander Wilson, and would actually say hello and give us all individual feedback, but he rarely discussed anything unrelated to the lesson, unlike Dr Lewis, with whom we could talk about anything.

That day, he had us doing circuit training. The Elders had already vastly improved our health and fitness, it was a big focus for them. It was tiring, but it didn't help take my mind off everything that was going on. I thought about Michael and what he had done for me over the years; how he took me under his wing and always looked out for me. Dread rushed over me, and I started getting upset at the thought of never seeing him again. Trying to calm my thoughts, I reminded myself I still didn't know anything. I felt angry with myself for carrying on as normal, but also angry with him for not telling me what he was doing.

All I wanted to know was where Michael was and why he had disappeared. Was his miniature showdown with Commander Wilson really the reason he'd left? Was it a snap decision? Or was it something he had planned for a long time? I just hoped I would have the opportunity to ask him.

23

I lumbered back to the canteen with Joe, and we joined the food queue. It looked like beef stew, though I wasn't really paying attention. I was taking long breaks in between mouthfuls and chewing slowly; I didn't really have an appetite, but knew I needed the food for energy. I was moving the food around my plate as if I might find an answer under a piece of meat or vegetable. The awful feeling in the pit of my stomach was making eating difficult. Joe must have felt the same as he hardly touched his food either. He put down his knife and fork, took a sip of water and looked at me.

'Do you think we'll see Michael again?'

'I'm really not sure. You?'

'I hope so. I was thinking of visiting the hospital after dinner, I thought maybe he had checked himself in. He took a big fall and landed flat on his back. Maybe it was still hurting? I don't know, it's a long shot, isn't it?'

I swallowed my food and for the first time today gave something that resembled a smile. 'That's a great idea, Joe.'

'Really?' Joe wasn't used to getting compliments and looked unsure how to take it, though he sat a bit taller.

Just as I started to feel a sense of optimism for my friend, the doors to the canteen swung open and several Elders marched in. Everyone sat still, silent, instantly stopping what they were doing. I couldn't recall a time when I had seen so many Elders in the canteen. Each one wore a plain black armband, which I had never seen before, and took long, confident strides around the room. They were moving quickly. Before I knew it, they had surrounded the whole canteen, evenly spread apart, facing us with their arms by their sides, each holding their orb in their right hand. I was sure if any of us dared to move, they would have sprung to life and eliminated us.

I didn't have time to feel scared – it happened so quickly. The Elder at the front of the room took a step forward, placing a metal bar on the floor which projected an image of Michael. Joe and I looked at each other, fear in our eyes and our sense of optimism quickly disappearing.

The Elder began speaking, its voice filling the room. 'Good evening. At 8:30 a.m. this morning, this man, Michael Anderson, failed to report to his morning session and has not been seen since. This is a severe breach. He is not considered dangerous, however, we advise you not to approach him. Should you see him, or learn any information as to his whereabouts, you must come straight to an Elder. Michael Anderson needs to be held accountable for his actions. To be clear: if you come to us with information, you will not be putting yourself in any danger. However, if it is discovered that you are hiding information, being dishonest, or are in any way involved with this man's disappearance, it will be treated as a crime. As with any crime, we only have one form of punishment.

'From day one, we have ruled fairly and honestly, which is why we treat criminal activity so severely. As far as we are concerned, there is no such thing as a minor crime – only crime. I can assure you, this man will be found, and he will be dealt with. Enjoy your evening.'

The Elder paused for a second, as if giving the room a few seconds to remember Michael's face, before turning off the bar and exiting the room. The other Elders filtered out in military fashion, identically paced. They were exceptionally well trained.

Now we knew for certain that Michael wasn't in one of the hospitals. Once again, in a matter of seconds, everything had changed. The feeling of hope had now completely vanished, replaced by a feeling of grim inevitability.

If Michael was still alive, it wouldn't be for long.

24

People in the room slowly began to speak, as if someone was gradually turning up the volume. You could hear gossiping, and people were questioning what had just happened. No one had gone missing before. Most people seemed baffled as to where he could be, coming up with their own theories. There were those who were alarmed and scared for Michael, his disappearance reopening old wounds and bringing back memories that had been pushed far back, too painful to reopen. Others appeared energised, almost excited that they had something different to talk about. Joe and I continued to sit in silence, deep in thought, trying to keep our emotions under control.

'What's going on, Joe?' My voice wobbled, my emotions starting to bubble over. It was now me who needed some reassurance.

'This is all wrong, Jack. I don't know why this is happening, but I need to get out of here.' Joe looked uncomfortable, fidgeting while looking around as if all eyes were on him.

'I agree. This is horrible. Everyone seems to think he's dead already.' My voice was rough.

I felt sick and didn't have the energy to say or even think of anything encouraging. Neither of us were touching our food; we were both trying to hear what people were saying, intently listening to everything going on around us. Everyone was coming to the same conclusion, which didn't help either of us.

'I think I'm going to find my family, Jack. I'll see you tomorrow.'

'Of course, I'll come out with you.'

We both got up with difficulty, the physical and mental toll of the day had now hit with all its force.

We went outside and shook hands goodbye. It was formal and awkward; we both felt uneasy, but a hug would have felt like we had given up, which we weren't ready to do.

'See you, Jack. Please don't do anything stupid tonight.' Joe gripped my hand, a note of desperation in his voice I had never heard.

I nodded reassuringly. 'Don't worry, I won't. Take care of yourself. I'll see you tomorrow.'

I stood alone, watching Joe walk away like I was hypnotised. I let out a big sigh, trying to release the bad energy and thoughts from my body. I needed to speak to Mum, but didn't feel ready. I was being a coward, too afraid to see her face. I didn't want to see David either. Though he was my oldest and best friend, I couldn't burden him with my troubles, not when he had a young family to worry about.

I looked at the hut where the lanterns were kept. I knew who I was going to see. Amy had always been there for me, and I needed her now. She was rational and mature; I knew she would know what to do, and selfishly, I didn't want to be alone with my thoughts, my imagination spiralling out

of control. I found her company calming and familiar –
even if she couldn't help, she would still make me feel at
least a little better.

I went into the hut, collected a lantern, and signed
out, grateful we were still allowed to leave. I wasn't stupid
though, I knew how closely they'd be watching me. The
Elders knew I was close to Michael, they were probably
hoping I was about to lead them to him. I wondered how
quickly we'd be put into lockdown when they realised I
knew as little as they did.

The route to Amy's town was like David's in terms of
terrain and length. I focused on getting there as fast as
possible; I wasn't really taking in any of my surroundings
or acknowledging any of the people I saw along the way, I
just wanted to see Amy. We didn't have mobile phones so
there was no way of arranging a place to meet, but I had
a good idea where she would be – the New Life District
where Amy would spend most of her evenings with her
sister.

I arrived at Rebecca's house and knocked on the door.
If Amy wasn't here, Rebecca would know where she was.
Once I heard the cheerful cry of "come in", I poked my
head past the door. I had got it right first time.

Amy and Rebecca sat on one bed, with two-year-old
Robert asleep on the other. He looked peaceful, so I was
careful not to wake him.

'Hi, guys,' I whispered from across the room. Neither of
them looked surprised to see me. 'Rebecca, do you mind if
I steal your sister for a bit?'

Rebecca smiled broadly, her smile so bright she could

light up a whole room. 'No problem,' she whispered back.

Amy leaned over, giving her sister a quick hug before getting up and leaving with me.

We sat outside on the grass about ten metres from Rebecca's. It was still warm and pleasant out, even though the sun had started its descent. The clouds were light and stretched along the sky, which was painted an array of pinks, oranges and yellows. Amy put her arm around me and pulled me close, not because it was cold, but to offer her support. We sat briefly in silence before Amy spoke. It turned out she already knew the reason for my spontaneous visit. She told me the Elders had stormed the canteens in her town at dinnertime to announce Michael's disappearance (they must have done the same in all the local districts). Although Michael and Amy only ever saw each other when she came to visit me, she recognised his name and face instantly.

Amy went on to ask why he had done it? Where would he go? Did I know anything?

I found myself saying, 'I don't know,' a lot.

Amy was satisfied to hear I wasn't involved and admitted that was her biggest fear. She didn't want me to try to protect him and get myself in trouble.

We soon found ourselves reflecting on the past few years and what we had lost and given up along the way. I wasn't sure if she had deliberately moved the subject on to take my mind off everything, but the conversation continued to flow seamlessly.

We both remained nostalgic about "the good old days". No matter what horrors we faced, our memories were our own and we wouldn't let those become rotten. Often, we would reminisce about Laura and Tom, dreaming of being carefree children again. The world had changed so much, yet she and I had remained the same.

I could have sat there with her all night, but knew it was only fair to let Amy return to her sister. Besides, I had a curfew to get back for. Before leaving, Amy asked me to make sure I looked after myself, which I said I would, and had every intention of doing. Though the visit had been short, it had been a helpful conversation. "A problem shared is a problem halved" as the saying goes.

I finally arrived home, glad to be leaving the day behind me. I knew there was still one person I needed to speak to. There was a sombre atmosphere to the dorm; people were talking, but being respectful, speaking softly, no howls of laughter nor shouting, almost like a vigil. The main lights were out, but people had dotted lanterns around the room. Some were sat around them like a campfire, sharing stories, while others were just relaxing on their beds, staring at their light as if it held the solution to all their woes. I stood looking at the people sat together in solidarity and, for the first time that day, I had a warm feeling. Despite everything we had been through, people still found comfort from one another. As long as we had each other, there was something to live for; a future to believe in. At times like this, it was important I kept reminding myself of that.

Mum was sitting on her bed folding clothes. I moved towards her calmly, taking light steps so I didn't make too much noise. Mum had a lantern on the bed that left a circle of light on the floor around her. I took a step into the light, as if entering her room. Mum looked up, her face alight with relief when she saw me. Without saying a word, she wrapped her arms around me tightly. It was exactly what I needed. For a moment, my stress lifted and I felt safe and at ease, as if any problem in the world could be solved. Even an eighteen-year-old could find reassurance in a mother's hug.

'It's okay,' she whispered as she pulled away, looking directly into my eyes trying to comfort me.

'I don't know what to do, Mum, I don't know anything.'

'I know, Jack, which is for the best. You heard what the Elders said. Don't you worry about Michael. He's strong.'

'I just want Michael to be alright, but I don't know how he can be.'

'I know.' Mum hugged me again; she knew there was nothing she could say to make it better. She just wanted to be there for me and be strong for the both of us. She was doing an amazing job.

We let each other go, smiling sadly. Whatever was going to happen tomorrow or the day after that, I knew I had Mum, and that was heartening.

I collapsed onto my bed and looked to my right to see Michael's empty bed in the dark corner, untouched for over twenty-four hours. It looked lonely and lost, and I hoped Michael was in better circumstances. I squeezed my eyes shut and lay there on my back. I was trying to focus on clearing my mind, but I had extracts from the day playing in my head, as if on repeat. I kept replaying the moment when we realised Michael wasn't turning up; I could see the Elders walking into the canteen to pronounce Michael missing. It was constant, and as I relived these moments in my head, I was having the same feelings I had earlier in the day, as if it was happening all over again. My body was stiff with anxiety and my heart was beating so hard I could almost hear it.

I just wanted to be asleep, if it was only for a few hours, to momentarily release me from these feelings.

25

The next day hit me out of nowhere like a steam train, the sound of my alarm an instant reminder of everything that was going on in the waking world. I got out of bed and lumbered my way through my morning ritual. Mentally, I wasn't sure where I was. With the invasion, everything had happened so quickly, our fate had already been decided. We didn't have time to over think it – it was all about survival – but with this, it was the not knowing that was the hardest to deal with. I didn't know if I would see Michael today, tomorrow or ever again. And I didn't know if or when I would learn anything about his whereabouts, and if I did, it would probably be bad news. The lack of sleep from the night before and the stress of the last twenty-four hours were taking their toll on me and I felt as if I was coming down with the flu.

The weirdest part of the situation was that the whole day went by again completely ordinarily, as if nothing was happening. It wasn't just expected, it was imperative to go through the day as if it was just the same as every other. Joe and I were still quiet and attempted to avoid talking about Michael despite it being the only thing either of us could think about. The day passed with nothing of note happening; life couldn't be back to normal already, surely?

I ate dinner with Joe. I must have looked over at the

door a hundred times, half expecting the Elders to storm in to say where Michael was, but it never happened. After dinner, I decided to use the evening to speak to Dr Lewis, so I made my way back to the Learning District. It was still warm, not a single cloud in the sky. The sun had begun its descent, and the buildings were leaving long shadows across the ground.

There was no one else around. The Learning District was always a ghost town at this time of day, lessons all complete. I was getting closer to Dr Lewis's classroom, walking down the pathway with classrooms to my left and right in neat rows, each one empty. My mind was as vacant as the buildings, my head tilted to the floor, looking at the shadows. Each one was perfectly clear and like an elongated, abstract black painting.

In the middle of the main gate was a shadow of someone, or something. I looked up to see who it was, but the sun was behind the figure, turning it into a dark silhouette. The silhouette was too tall to be a human. It took a step towards me and though all the Elders looked the same, I had a bad feeling in the pit of my stomach that I knew this one.

The red armband confirmed it was Commander Wilson.

I had not seen him in the Learning District since the invasion, so seeing him here now made me feel particularly uneasy (change was rarely a good thing these days). I took a big gulp and tried to control my heart rate, reminding myself that I had done nothing wrong, but even so, I made a deliberate attempt to look as unsuspicious as possible.

With each step I took towards Dr Lewis's classroom, he took a step towards me.

I was now standing in his shadow, still a few metres away from him, but he must have been able to hear my nervous breathing.

'Jack Palmer.'

He knew my name. This was not good at all.

I cleared my throat. 'Yes, Commander?'

'Where is Michael Anderson.'

'I swear I don't know anything. I haven't seen him.'

I attempted to act natural and carried on walking, trying to get past the intimidating figure of Commander Wilson, but he took a step to his right, blocking off my path. This conversation wasn't over yet.

'Then why is your heart rate so fast and breathing so heavy? You are also struggling to keep eye contact. These are all clear signs that you are lying.'

'I'm sorry, Commander Wilson, you just caught me by surprise, and I've been worried about Michael. This conversation is making me a little anxious, but I promise you, I don't know anything.' I tried to take another step around him.

'You expect me to believe that?'

Without emotion, he effortlessly shoved me to the floor. I had never seen an Elder touch a human, they always used the orbs. The path was dusty and hard, and I felt myself slide, the concrete taking the skin off my right leg and hand. Both were stinging, but right now, I had more important things to worry about.

'I promise you I don't know anything. If I did, I would

tell you.' Desperation was evident in my voice and I made no attempt to get up, for fear of looking confrontational.

'You expect me to believe that, Jack Palmer? Humans are weak, he would have had to consult with someone. From my knowledge and understanding, you were his closest friend, so it would have been you. However smart you think you are, you would do well not to forget that you are a speck of dust in comparison to me.'

'Commander, please, I don't know anything. Look at me! If I did, I would say, wouldn't I?' I willed him to believe me with every fibre of my being.

I felt like I could see each individual muscle in his shoulder moving and pulsing, his triceps almost popping out of his arms. He wore his muscles like armour; the Elders had made themselves look like the perfect species. In a fist fight, I knew there was absolutely no way I could win.

'Lying to an Elder and preventing justice is a crime, Jack Palmer. Your friend Michael Anderson disrespected me, and I let him go out of pity. I won't be making the same mistake again.'

Out of seemingly nowhere, he produced his orb and gripped it menacingly.

'Please, Commander…' This wasn't how I expected it to end, lying on the floor covered in dust like a coward. The last time I had felt this hopeless I was sitting on the floor of my bathroom and had just lost my father and sister.

'So be it.'

I looked up at Commander Wilson, and I could see my shrinking reflection in his huge eyes. There was no remorse there, no element of doubt, nothing. Just me.

I looked down at the floor, ready to face the inevitable. A second passed, but I was still there.

I looked up.

There was another Elder with him. I recognised the blue band. My friend, Dr Lewis, had hold of Commander Wilson's arm, the one holding the orb.

'We don't kill innocent people, Commander,' Dr Lewis insisted.

'He isn't innocent, Doctor, he is withholding information, and for that reason, he needs to be terminated.'

Though externally identical in every way, on the inside, they were total opposites; even without the armbands, I would have known who was who.

'He is innocent. I won't allow this.'

Though Commander Wilson's left arm remained in Dr Lewis's vice-like grip, the furious Elder moved his free arm to strike Dr Lewis in the head, but he managed to duck and send a counter punch into the commander's ribs.

I had never seen them fight. Now, I was watching two of them scrap like animals, the outcome probably deciding whether I lived or died. They were built like titans, warring blow for blow, throwing punches, grappling and using their orbs like a weapon to strike each other.

Neither would give in. Commander Wilson was beginning to win, Dr Lewis having to defend. I was still on the floor, a mere spectator, stunned at what was going on in front of my eyes. Commander Wilson was throwing more punches and landing more blows, clearly hurting Dr Lewis, though they were both beginning to bruise and graze, with cuts starting to appear on their bodies and faces. They were looking vulnerable, almost like humans.

Commander Wilson wrestled with Dr Lewis, then landed a combination of punches to his side and face. He looked as if he was beginning to set himself up for the killer blow.

Dr Lewis, now in Hail Mary territory, swung a huge, sharp punch, landing it on Commander Wilson's jaw, which made him stumble back a few paces, visibly dazed. Just before he managed to compose himself and re-join the fight, Dr Lewis used his orb, quickly lifting his right arm and shooting Commander Wilson.

Within a split second, it was over.

Commander Wilson was gone.

Dr Lewis stood there, the victor, with a deep cut around his right eye and bruises all over his body.

I owed him my life.

He picked up Commander Wilson's orb, the only remnant of the once powerful leader, and stood, the sun behind him, looking down at me like a hero.

'Come with me, Jack.'

26

I stood and brushed myself down, inspecting the graze on my knee and hand before sheepishly following Dr Lewis into his classroom. My grazes were utterly insignificant compared to the injuries my saviour had sustained. He went over to his desk and sat, leaning forward onto the table, trying to gather his composure. He had taken many strikes to the head and was clearly concussed. I grabbed a chair on my way over to his desk and placed it on the opposite side. I sat, wondering whether it was better to give Dr Lewis space or help him.

'Are you okay?' I asked, knowing he wasn't.

Dr Lewis sat up and pulled out a black box from his desk drawer, clumsily throwing it in front of him. He was shaking. He opened the box, withdrawing a syringe with yellow liquid in it. He planted the needle straight into his arm, injecting himself with the liquid before leaning back in his chair.

'I'm okay. We always keep an emergency recovery pack in our rooms.'

His wounds were healing in front of my eyes, the grazes slowly disappearing as if being absorbed by his body. The cut round his eye was quickly being replaced by fresh skin. Within a matter of seconds, it was as if he had never been in such a brutal fight at all. I leaned forward in awe, amazed at what I had just seen. I knew their medicine was advanced, but not this much.

Something niggled at my brain as I watched his injuries heal. Something small, too insubstantial to grab hold of and understand, but it was important. What was I missing?

'How is that possible?' I asked.

Dr Lewis was now sitting comfortably and began speaking in his robotic voice. 'You wouldn't understand, Jack. There is a lot you don't understand. Remember, this isn't our actual form.'

'I know, but the cuts and bruises were real, surely? You looked in pain.'

'Correct, the flesh and wounds are real; it isn't a mask or costume, this is my current form. When we invented a way to manipulate the way we look and to change our bodies in every way, we also discovered ways to speed up the healing process and how to regenerate the broken cells. It was essential when we began space travel to disguise our actual appearance to protect our own species. This prevented planets knowing how we looked and knowing what our weaknesses were. It also helped in making ourselves approachable to the specific planet. At the first meeting, we never wish to strike fear or cause confusion as our plan wouldn't work. But yes, we are still mortal like humans, the pain and wounds are real. But now they are gone.'

I sat there, momentarily stunned, unsure why he had told me this. 'What about Commander Wilson? Surely Elders will begin looking for him?'

'Not publicly. For the plan to work, we need the home species to believe us to be indestructible, a superior being.

We have to educate and lead. We have a specific hierarchy. You need to believe we have no weaknesses, that you are inferior to us. We are all identical, so tomorrow, no human except you will know that Commander Wilson has gone. Another Elder will take over his post under the same name and act the same way. That is the job of the district leader.'

I realised Dr Lewis was telling me more than he should; I had learnt more in two minutes than any history lesson.

'You said "for the plan to work"… what plan?'

Dr Lewis sat for a moment in silence, as if preparing the words in his head, looking at me. 'I have been waiting to tell you this for a long time, Jack. Now, I believe you are ready.'

I held my breath. This was big.

He leaned forward, resting his forearms on the table, linking his hands together. 'I do not know where Michael is or what he is doing. It seems unlikely we will see him alive again. Commander Wilson is not involved either, though he did come for you because of Michael. It was just a coincidence that I heard you from my room talking to each other.' He paused, seeming to sigh. 'No, this is much bigger than Michael and Commander Wilson; it is bigger than you and me. It's about the future of humanity.'

The light outside was beginning to dull, everything in the room turning a shade of grey. It was quiet and eerie. Normally, I wouldn't like to be here at this time; if something was to happen to me, no one would know. But I was so intrigued with what Dr Lewis was about to say, I would have stayed all night if I had to. He leaned under his desk, pulling out a lantern and placing it between us and turning it on. He had my full attention.

'It began thousands of years ago, with political parties debating about our defences and how best to protect our planet. Our planet is large, twenty times larger than Earth. We are also an old and advanced species, and had always felt safe, knowing what we did about the universe. But at that time, we had recently discovered larger, more advanced planets. One political party was determined that we needed a defence strategy, should these planets try to invade us.

'For the first time, fear spread across our planet like a disease, and a dangerous one at that. Their strategy gained traction amongst the public, and it was agreed that we would shift our attention from health and education to creating weapons and discovering new planets, learning which were weaker than ours so that we could invade and create colonies. This would improve our numbers, as we could recruit inhabitants from these planets to fight for us, resulting in fewer casualties of our own species. They wanted to turn us into a war machine.'

I was stunned, trying to digest the information. 'But if you put weapons in the hands of humans, we wouldn't fight for you. You killed our loved ones and took away our freedom.'

Dr Lewis nodded. 'Correct, you would not fight for us, Jack. But this is a long-term project. Elders live on average seven hundred human years. Your generation knows about life before we came to your planet, but generations down the line? All they will know is that we took away your wars, we eradicated disease and made you healthy, we helped restore the planet you nearly destroyed, we kept you safe, and we are a more powerful, caring creature from a far-off planet. They will not even know there was an invasion. You will not fight for us, your children will not even fight for us, maybe even *their* children will not fight for us, but we are rewriting human history. Soon, humanity will not know any different. They will be like machines, never stepping out of line. They will worship us like gods and be willing to die for us.

'Why do you think we prioritise children, and make it more appealing to live in the New Life Districts? We don't just allow reproduction, we encourage it. Even now, you can see people in the New Life District who are happy and accept their way of life. We need you to keep reproducing and continue being happy, as by doing so you are creating an army for us. We have hundreds of planets like this all over the universe and you are only a small part of the puzzle, but a part nonetheless. Soon, we will be able to attack planets hundreds of times the size of this one without risking a single one of our species.'

Dr Lewis hadn't broken eye contact throughout the whole speech. He was an Elder I trusted, but what he was telling me was terrifying.

I sat back, moving away from the light, my hands over my face. I still had more questions that needed answering. My voice was stuttering, my brain working faster than my mouth. 'So, you are willing to kill us off for your war? A whole species?'

'If it means protecting our own, then yes. We could send a hundred species into war and lose every single one of them, win the war and not suffer a single fatality of our own.'

It was a simple, logical answer to such a complex question.

'I don't understand, the invasion only started because a human killed Professor Watson. Or was that not…' I trailed off as the truth hit me. *That* was what I'd been trying to understand as I'd observed Dr Lewis healing his injuries. A simple gunshot couldn't kill an Elder. Their technology was far too advanced.

'It was staged, all of it. Think back to that night. Do you think a human would have been able just to walk past security, get onto the stage unimpeded, and kill Professor Watson? Of course not. We can change form, remember? The invasions need to be strategic. We need the main species of the inhabited planet to understand and not fear us. We need to make ourselves look peaceful. The first contact cannot be the invasion, it must look as if it was our only choice and the fault of the inhabitant species. By doing so, they will be more cooperative from the beginning and grateful to be alive. Not to mention the fact it minimises the risk that they will be prepared for a full-scale invasion. Once this act is done, we then destroy everything as quickly as possible and start afresh. It has only been a few years and already people speak with the Elders and accept their life. Very few people viscerally hate us. This is all part of the plan.'

Dr Lewis was telling me everything, as if confessing to all of the Elders' crimes over the years. I didn't know what he was hoping to achieve. My head was a mess. How had we been so stupid? It wasn't that I hadn't questioned this before; we'd just never had a chance to. One shot, one bullet... one staged bullet to make the Elders' cause seem noble and worthy, like they were the peacekeepers. Yet, in reality, they were nothing more than invaders. And their endgame? To create an army of loyal followers.

My brain instantly went to my sister and father, to everyone who had lost someone. 'So, the invasion wasn't our fault?'

'No. We were in control of the whole thing. It was all staged to start a war.'

'Why are you telling me all this?'

'It goes back to the political parties. As I said, fear spread across the planet and a large portion of the population wanted these plans to go ahead. However, the other political party completely opposed the idea. They argued we had always been peaceful and cared about discovering new life and bettering ourselves, not about conquering. Another large portion of the planet agreed with these views, and the political debates raged on, turning into a civil war which engulfed our planet for many years. The irony is, we were arguing about how best to protect our planet whilst we nearly destroyed it ourselves.

'When the war finally came to an end, it was decided that we would go ahead with the new weapons and space program. A law was passed that everyone would have to do a minimum of two hundred years' service to either program. Refusal would result in the death penalty. There was nowhere to hide; everyone had to do their service for their planet. The political party that opposed the idea disappeared for their own safety. They were prisoners on their own planet.'

'Prisoners on their own planet? I can't imagine what *that* feels like,' I said bitterly.

'What if I told you there was a way to get Earth back?'

What? I frowned up at Dr Lewis. 'How?'

'A thousand years ago, we were invading a planet in our usual strategic way. We studied them, knew everything about them, and were prepared to take it. They had no space program, no intention of travelling into the unknown, they had never even discussed it. We named them Rock Huggers and thought it would be straightforward. They were all trained to fight from birth, but we never saw them go into battle; they never went to war with each other. They were less intelligent than us and we thought it would be an easy takeover. Little did we know that their training was all in preparation for fighting back. The planet was hot, but they had thick scales to protect them. It was also bright, as the planet was close to a star, but they had small eyes to protect and aid their vision.

'For the first time, an invasion failed. Their eyes were unaffected by the orb's powers, so we were unable to send them into unconsciousness, and in close combat, we were unequipped to compete. There were questions of scrapping the whole thing, but it was decided this was a one-off failing and we would continue. But in the fallout of the failure, a small group of rebels came together. They have been hiding in secret ever since, trying to develop a plan to scrap the space and weapons program and go back to the way we were meant to be – peaceful. I, Jack, am part of that Resistance.'

I was shaking my head as if I could rid his words from my brain; just by knowing this information I was being put in danger. 'You shouldn't be telling me this. I still don't understand why you are.'

'Jack, we failed to successfully invade a planet, and we almost scrapped the program. If we lose another planet The Resistance will have a strong case. Our numbers will grow, and we can go back to our home planet and re-open the debate. I want humans to win back Earth.'

'But how?'

'You and I go to the Rock Huggers' planet and convince them to fight for the humans. We already have the rebellious Elders and humans on our side. With the aid of the Rock Huggers, we would be too powerful for the remaining Elders on Earth and could tip the odds in our favour.'

Dr Lewis made the plan seem easy.

'Why are you bringing this to me? What can I do that you can't?' It seemed as if Dr Lewis had spilled the secrets of his species for absolutely no reason.

'A human needs to be there, it gives us a superior chance at success. To show them that two species can work together, that humans can trust Elders, despite it all.'

I shook my head. 'Maybe so, but… still… why me?'

Dr Lewis was staring right at me; I could see my reflection in his bulbous eyes. I was a young man, no more than a boy, really. Surely there was someone more qualified than me; braver, stronger?

'I have been chosen as the Elder to complete this

mission, and I have chosen you, Jack. I know you, I trust you, and I believe in you.'

I let that sink in. He trusted me. But did I trust him? So much had happened that suggested I shouldn't. But he had also saved my life; killed one of his own for my sake.

'Last time aliens came to Earth, it didn't really go well for us humans. I can't be responsible for another invasion. How do you know they would fight for us, anyway? You said they aren't interested in space travel.'

'I don't know that they would. But I personally have nothing to lose. There is only so long that The Resistance can work in secret. All I do know is if we don't try, the human race is as good as over. Together, we can show them species from different planets can work together for a greater cause, start something bigger than both of us, bigger than this planet.'

I sat momentarily in silence. Two days ago, my life was normal and consistent. But now, Michael had disappeared, I had nearly been killed, I had witnessed an Elder kill another, and had just been told everything had been based on a lie and that humans were doomed. Oh, and there was a way I could potentially save the entire human race. What was I meant to say to that?

'Do you have a plan?' I eventually asked.

'Yes,' Dr Lewis replied, not elaborating any further.

I got up slowly, putting my chair back in its original place behind a table. Dr Lewis was still sitting behind his desk, watching my every step. The room was dark except for him, bathed in a circle of light. I didn't have a lantern, but at this point in time, I felt safer in the dark. I already knew more than I wanted to, and I wasn't ready to hear his plan. I suddenly became acutely aware that he was an Elder, who had an orb, who had just revealed his species' darkest secrets – I no longer felt safe being here.

'I'm sorry, I need time to think about this, this is all too much for me.'

It wasn't the answer he was hoping for.

'I understand, Jack. I hope you know not to tell anyone any of the information I have shared with you today. Not only would you be in grave danger, you would also put any people you share this knowledge with in danger.'

'I know. And… thank you, for saving my life,' I added as an afterthought.

Dr Lewis nodded his acknowledgement as he watched me leave his classroom, now armed with the truth.

I replayed the conversation with Dr Lewis in my mind repeatedly through the night, hardly believing it had really happened. Why had he come to me with this? I wasn't special, and I didn't want to be a hero. I had unwillingly been thrust into something I didn't want to be a part of. It was bigger than me, it was bigger than anyone: it was bigger than the world. How was I meant to comprehend something so large?

I went through my morning schedule on muscle memory alone. I didn't even know Dr Lewis's full plan, but couldn't foresee a situation where it would work and we would get our planet back. Even if we did, it could never be the *same* planet that we lost all those years ago. There was no reason for any other planets out there to want to help us. I could see hundreds of scenarios where it wouldn't work, where I wouldn't be coming back, where I wouldn't see Mum, David or Amy again. But, at the same time, if I didn't at least *try*, what did that say about me? We might never get back to where we were pre-invasion, but at least we could be free.

I was tense on my way to the canteen, walking around like I was guilty of something, avoiding eye contact with everyone. I sat by myself, not because I was ignoring people, but because I didn't trust myself not to say something. I couldn't sit with Mum – she would be able to tell something was wrong (I wasn't a good liar). I ate my breakfast as quickly as possible and made my way to the meeting point for building. I arrived very early, but I didn't mind. I wasn't really thinking about time. I just stood, unseeing, staring into the middle distance.

'Jack?'

I shook my head and blinked hard, trying to shake myself out of the trance I was in. I turned around and saw Joe, a bemused expression on his face.

'Are you okay?' he asked apprehensively.

'Yeah, I'm fine,' I answered, deliberately evasive, not wanting to give anything away. It probably made me look even more suspicious.

Joe stared accusingly at me as if he was aware I was hiding something. 'Just thinking about Michael, are you?' He put a supportive hand on my shoulder.

I was over-thinking everything. But then I *did* feel guilty, because I hadn't thought about Michael once this morning... I had much bigger things to worry about.

'Yeah, something like that,' I responded, nodding at Joe as if pleading for him to believe me.

'You look stressed, mate. You know, if you need someone to talk to, you can come to me.'

Joe was being friendly and thoughtful, but all I wanted was for this conversation to be over. I probably did look stressed. I felt like I was under an intense amount of pressure. My body felt tight and my face puffy, I was unshaven and probably had bags under my eyes from sleep-deprivation.

I put on my best fake smile and began to make my excuses. 'Thanks. I woke up with a bit of a headache and I've not been sleeping too well, you know, with everything going on.'

Joe seemed to believe me as he nodded understandingly.

An Elder turned up for us to check in. Just as Dr Lewis had said would happen, he wore Commander Wilson's armband. There was absolutely no reason for anyone to suspect this wasn't Commander Wilson, but I knew the truth. This new Elder stood in the same way as every other Elder, with great posture, confidence and authority. I had seen Commander Wilson be eliminated with my own eyes and even I was questioning whether this was him or an imposter. I had to get control of myself. I was questioning everything and could feel my thoughts spiralling out of control. It was a peculiar feeling, knowing something everyone else didn't, and I wasn't handling it very well.

The only aspect of my day that had changed was my thought process. I didn't want to be building or at lessons, I wanted answers, but I knew I didn't have a choice. All my choices had been removed. I was analysing everything and trying to piece everything together in my mind, but nothing would fit.

After dinner, which I had also eaten by myself, I decided to go straight to bed to avoid talking to anyone. I desperately wanted to speak to Amy, but knew I wouldn't be able to resist telling her everything and it wouldn't be right to endanger her life just to clear my own head.

I lay in bed with my eyes glued shut. My bed didn't feel comfortable at all; my body felt too rigid. I kept moving around, but no position was working. All I could see was darkness, but all my other senses were still switched on. I could hear people talking and laughing around the room. If they knew what I did, they wouldn't be in such high spirits.

It was true that people with clearer minds slept better, and mine had never been murkier. I was torturing myself over the decisions I still faced. My eyelids were getting droopier, but I kept waking myself up in fear that an Elder was standing over me, ready to take me away. It was hard to tell if this was a vivid nightmare or an overactive imagination. I lay there, simultaneously cold and sweating, but I wasn't ill: I was stressed.

It must have been nearly morning by the time I finally fell asleep. I knew this pattern couldn't continue.

28

Time had no meaning to me. While I had this hanging over my head, time didn't seem to move; it was just this consistent and ever-present feeling that the next second could change my life.

The only thing that seemed to help was seeing a friendly face. After I'd managed to keep Dr Lewis's secret for the whole of the first day, I'd become slightly more confident in my secret-keeping abilities and had started to talk to people again. Sitting with Mum and Julie at mealtimes had distracted me, the familiarity of their faces was a calming presence in what had been a whirlwind couple of days. They would natter away just as they always did, and though I offered little to the conversation, I didn't feel I needed to. We had all become so comfortable in each other's company, they didn't expect me to say much.

All the same, they had definitely noticed something was off, but so far, they hadn't pushed me. Whether they had realised I didn't want to (well, wasn't able to) talk about it, or whether they were just waiting for me to eventually open up, I wasn't sure, but I was grateful regardless.

One evening, as I sat with them, I rolled a carrot around my plate, waiting for the right time to put an end to its misery. I felt out of my depth, alone and completely helpless. I eventually stabbed my fork through the carrot and put it into my mouth.

'I was always a big lover of fish growing up,' I heard Julie say in her dulcet tone.

Her voice was gravelly, but I always enjoyed listening to it. She was taking small precise bites of her food, chewing for longer than normal as if she was really enjoying her meal today.

'Do you like fish, Jack?' she asked, unsubtly trying to bring me into the conversation.

'Yeah, I do.' My answer was void of expression.

'Feeling tired? Me too, age is catching up with me,' Julie added.

'Unless there's something else…?' Mum prompted.

At that moment the doors opened swiftly, letting in a flood of light. Everyone looked over in unison. It was the Elders again. They swarmed around the room exactly as they had before. A collective deep inhale of breath could be heard, before silence. Everyone knew they weren't coming in to deliver good news. Maybe time was going so slowly it had begun going backwards. It felt like I was reliving the exact same moment.

We sat silently and patiently as the Elders took their positions round the edge of the room, evenly spaced. They were standing tall as if creating a cage from which there was no escape. Whatever they were going to be saying would be heard. The silence was uncomfortable, everyone waiting like statues. The Elder standing at the front of the room, who appeared to be the leader of this troop, stepped forward, as if taking to the stage. They stood confidently, like they belonged, looking slowly around the room for effect, showing that even just the sight of an Elder could send a room into hyper-focus and silence.

'Good evening,' the voice was robotic but had a noticeably female tone, 'and apologies for disturbing your dinner. This will only take a few moments, but we felt it was important to share the recent developments in the Michael Anderson case.

'This afternoon, a report was sent from a town not too far from here that the man we have been searching for was spotted in a nearby woodland area. An Elder search party was sent to investigate further. I can confirm that the man was in fact Michael Anderson. The case has come to its swift and rightful conclusion: he was quickly apprehended and eliminated.'

Another collective breath, this time of shock. I had feared that this was how it would end, and deep down I had known this was the only way. But, in typical human fashion, I had been hanging on to that impossible belief that, in some miraculous way, Michael would be discovered and everything could return to normal. Having the news confirmed that he was gone hit me like a train: I could see it coming, but couldn't move out of the way.

I felt sick; lightheaded; my legs were going weak. I was glad I was sitting down. I clenched my fists as tightly as I could, as if gripping them hard enough would supress all the anger and pain inside me. On the outside, I gave no reaction, but on the inside, I was screaming. Michael was gone.

I would never see him again.

The Elder paused for a second time before continuing

their speech. 'I want everyone to know it was quick and efficient. This was not something we wanted to do, it is not something we enjoyed doing, but Michael Anderson had given us no choice. It was a waste of Elders' time and a waste of a human life. We are trying to better you as a species and we have seen great improvements, but the rules need to be followed. We have removed war and conflict from your planet, but you must remain focused and disciplined. It is important we learn from the past to improve our future. You need to understand that we are superior; that we know what is best for your planet. If you continue to obey our rules, you will survive. If not, you will be eliminated. Let this be a reminder to all of you.'

Once the Elder had finished their speech and stepped back, they all left the room in perfect harmony. They didn't even wait to see how the room reacted to the news.

I was angry at myself for allowing this to happen, for not trying harder to find Michael, for leaving him alone that night rather than sticking close to his side. Grief, fear, rage, self-loathing: they were all swirling inside my head, and I wasn't ready to deal with them.

The noise in the room was rising, everyone seemingly having something to say. My body was malfunctioning. I was sweating, my head was spinning and the sound was deafening. I felt as if I was about to collapse. I stood suddenly, feeling the rush of blood to my head. I was in trouble; the whole room was blurring. I stumbled to the door, bumping into numerous people along the way, my spatial awareness completely gone. The door swung open as I pushed through it with my shoulder. As soon as I hit fresh air, I stopped and leaned over with my hands on my knees, taking deep, exaggerated breaths to try to get oxygen pumping around my body. I stood up, searching my surrounding as if it was all brand new and confusing.

I felt something land on my shoulder.

'Jack.'

29

Mum had followed me out. She stood looking up at me, her face agonised, though she was trying to hide it. Her forehead was furrowed, her eyebrows hooded over eyes which were blazing with fury; sparkling with unshed tears. What was wrong with me? I hadn't even *thought* about the fact she had lost Michael too.

'Shall we take a walk?' she asked quietly.

My body had started to return to its default setting. I chewed my bottom lip, and I rubbed my hand on the back of my neck. I was trying to show I wasn't upset, a trait I had inherited from my dad. Thinking of him now just made me want to burst into tears.

I nodded in answer to her question, not wanting to speak. I knew my shaky voice would betray me.

We walked in the direction of the dorms, though we weren't really walking anywhere specifically. We were just taking a stroll, ambling along, each trying to figure out the right words to say. It had been silent for some time, but I was the first to speak, not because I had thought of anything brilliant to say but because I just wanted to say *something*. Mum was more experienced than me and knew that sometimes saying nothing could be just as powerful.

'Why would Michael do this? It doesn't make sense.'

Mum paused for a moment, collecting her thoughts.

After everything she had been through and everything she had lost, there was no reason for her to be this calm, but she was a strong person with a strong mind. She didn't torture herself in the same way I did, carrying problems around.

'I honestly don't know, Jack. I can't think where he would have been going. But when I think about his reasons for leaving, I understand. Michael existed here because that's what we all do – we just survive. But he stopped living a long time ago. He had been doing the same stuff every day for years, against his will, just because he was told to by those who had taken his family. That takes its toll on some people. Maybe he had just had enough and didn't want to do it anymore. I know you'll miss him, love. I'll miss him more than words can say. But the man we knew? That wasn't the real him. The real Michael died all those years ago with his family.' Mum spoke with confidence, as if this was a thought she had been having since he disappeared and was just waiting for the right time to say it out loud.

'Is that how you feel, too?' I asked in trepidation. I couldn't lose Mum as well.

'No. But I still have you. My wonderful boy.' She smiled warmly and squeezed my arm before continuing. 'Everyone is different. We all deal with trauma and grief in different ways. You either grow around it and learn to live with it, or you shrivel and harden and sink into it. Let it fester and turn to poison. Michael didn't *want* to learn to live with it. He was too angry. He was… just so angry.'

'Do you think about them often?'

Her eyes misted over. 'Every day. Do you?'

The question made me feel uncomfortable., and I found myself rubbing my thumbs against my first two fingers, then pulling at my ear. I was twitchy; wracked with guilt.

'I do, but not as often as I should.'

'It's okay not to think about them all the time, Jack. There isn't a set amount of time you are meant to think about them. Everyone had a different way of coping with grief.'

There was no one else around, only a few squawking birds for company. The only thing that could see us was the sun, and even that was now hiding behind the clouds. These parts of town had returned to their original green state. It was quiet and secluded; I could share a secret here and no one would hear except a few old trees. If there was ever going to be a time to share information, now would be it.

I stopped dead in my tracks, slamming on the breaks as if I had reached my destination. But I had forgotten to tell my passenger, so Mum didn't notice I wasn't right next to her. She continued to walk for a couple of steps before turning her head, as if to look at me to carry on our conversation. I had clearly taken her by surprise – her eyebrows were raised and a curious look had painted itself across her face.

'What is it?'

'I've got something I need to say, but I … I don't know how much I can say or… or how to tell you.' I knew Mum could keep a secret, but I didn't want to put her in danger. I would tell her just enough to get her opinion, I decided. The burden of knowledge was mine, and mine alone.

Mum was moving closer to me cautiously, like I was a wild animal she was afraid to startle. 'It's okay, Jack. I'm here to help, whatever it is.'

'What would you say if I told you I had the opportunity to make a real difference to this world, for humankind, but that it would be dangerous? I wouldn't know when I'd see you again.'

Mum looked at me; I could tell by her eyes she was trying to work out if I had gone completely crazy and was just too polite to say it.

'Is this anything to do with Michael?'

'No, it's nothing to do with Michael, but… I do think it could make a difference. I had to tell you – I couldn't just leave you without explanation. And I won't do it without your permission.'

Mum looked at me, the strict expression on her face reminiscent of one she had worn often when I was a cheeky pre-teen with too much energy and no self-restraint.

She began speaking in a sterner tone. 'Jack, you're a young man now, you can make your own choices. I've watched you grow up and go through so much. If we hadn't been invaded, I know you would have gone on to do great things. It sounds to me like this might be your chance to do just that. I've had to watch you living a life you weren't meant to, and it hasn't been easy, but you've always remained positive, and you always make smart decisions. You are kind, clever and thoughtful, so do what you think is best and right. Don't worry about me. I shouldn't be a part of your decision.'

Mum always had a way with words, but she was wrong

about one thing.

'Of course you're part of my decision. You're the most important thing in the world to me.'

She smiled then, emotion overtaking her at my frankness. We never spoke like this, not really. We'd been through so much together and yet we still found it hard to be completely open with one another.

'If it is my permission you want, then you have it, no questions asked. I trust you. Whatever you're doing, it must be important, and if you can't tell me anything, then don't. Whatever happens I'll always love you, the same way I still love Claire.'

I could feel tears brimming in my eyes as I enveloped her in a hug. 'I know, Mum. Thank you.'

Deep down, I think I had always known what I would do with the information Dr Lewis had given me, or at least what I wanted to do. Now that I knew there was no chance of seeing Michael again, and I had Mum's blessing, I felt as though the decision had been solidified in my mind. I wouldn't be able to let Joe, David or Amy know, of course, but that was something I would have to live with. If Dr Lewis was telling the truth, and I was as certain as I could be in this messed up world that he was, this path was the only chance humanity had of experiencing freedom again.

30

I sat on my bed contemplating the meaning of life (or something equally as intangible). The light outside was beginning to fade, but it was still quite early, so the main lights were on, keeping the room bright. I probably wouldn't be spending many more nights in here, and if I was to return, it would never be like this again, not for me, anyway. Michael had left, been found and killed, and if I was to fail, I would share the same fate. There wasn't a scenario whereby I would be welcomed back into society. Once I left, my whole life would change forever.

I could feel seeds of doubt entering my mind as I gazed across the room. Long gone were the days of going to sleep with the sounds of crying echoing around the room, people screaming with night terrors, or the sounds of feet slapping against the floor as someone made a run for it. Most people were satisfied with their lives now, or at least, they thought they were.

I could see Mum and Julie across the room perched on a bed, engaged in their favourite hobby: talking. I knew Mum wouldn't be confiding in Julie the news I had told her – it would just be idle chitchat – but it was gratifying to know that Mum had someone else she felt close to.

There were people scattered across the whole room taking part in the exact same activity as Mum and Julie.

In our downtime, I was getting the impression that people felt free. This *was* home after all; if I was to take a photo right now of what I could see, it wouldn't look like a room full of prisoners, but a holiday camp, a place people would go to hang out.

With these pictures and thoughts slipping into my head, I couldn't help but think that maybe this world wasn't so bad. Indeed, the world was good, and I was happy. I had things to keep me occupied, a roof over my head, food in my belly, and even a surprisingly comfortable bed. How had I never noticed how comfortable my bed was? This might be the most comfortable bed in the world.

War had ceased to exist; nature was flourishing without the burning of fossil fuels and deforestation; there was no more poverty or illness. Maybe I was being hasty, thinking of going away with Dr Lewis to change it all?

Just as these reservations made their way into my mind, I caught another glimpse of Michael's bed, abandoned like a hollow shrine. To others, it was just a bed, but to me it was a reminder of the man who had stood alongside me and was now gone. He hadn't committed a heinous crime; he wasn't dangerous. He had just broken an arbitrary rule and had been murdered as a result. They had killed him. The man who had looked out for me; who I had been lucky enough to call my friend.

It was like that famous saying: I had two wolves in my head, trying to battle it out, one fighting for me to go with Dr Lewis, the other opposed to it. Every time one seemed to get the upper hand, the other wolf would snap back, turning the odds in its favour. I had thought I was certain, but as I sat there, I realised this wasn't a simple yes or no decision. There was a big grey area and a lot of maybes.

If history had proven anything, it was that big decisions would never please everyone. I had to make the choice that was right for me. Twenty years down the line, I needed to be able to look back and say I did it for the right reasons. When the invasion first took place, everyone was distraught and families torn apart. Elders lead by fear, not respect. Time had made us accustomed to our new way of life, but that didn't make it right.

The pressure of making such a big decision alone was causing me to doubt myself, making me anxious. I ran my hand over my face, closing my eyes and trying to focus my mind. It was then that a memory came to me, of something that I had been told many years ago. "Humans take two seconds upon receiving information to decide exactly how they are going to react".

I had known immediately that I had to go with Dr Lewis. Time and fear had just made me doubt that gut instinct.

I needed to go with my gut and not think about it anymore. Yes, humanity wasn't perfect; our lives before the invasion hadn't been perfect. But we deserved the chance to live as free people and right our own wrongs.

Just as the two wolves in my head stopped tussling, a familiar figure walked towards me. David now had such a big frame he lumbered everywhere. You wouldn't want to get in his way: if he picked up enough speed, it would be like being hit by a car.

Today, he didn't have his usual cheesy grin drawn across

his face. Instead, he looked mournful. He must have found out about Michael. As much as our friendship was based on having a laugh, in my times of need, he was always ready to comfort and look after me.

He perched on the end of the bed and sat in silence, just looking at me. For all his good nature, he couldn't find the right words to say, but him being there was enough for me. I didn't really want to talk about Michael's death anyway. It wasn't going to make me feel any better, so there was no need to pass any burden onto David. He had a young family and enough to think about.

I asked him how Josh was, and he instantly recognised that I wanted to keep things light.

'He's growing up so fast,' David remarked wistfully.

'It's crazy, really, especially since his dad still hasn't managed to!'

'Ha! That's rich coming from you.'

I chuckled. 'I don't think either of us were ever destined to grow up.'

'Speak for yourself.' Dave grinned. 'Ah, but we had a fun childhood, didn't we? We used to have so much energy, and get up to all sorts of mischief.'

'Nah, mate, *you* did. Putting up with you used up all my energy!'

'Another shot fired! Alright, I admit I was a pain, but it was all good fun, wasn't it?'

I grinned at him. 'That it was.'

'I just hope I can give Josh the same kind of childhood. Well, it won't be the same, of course not. But I want him to have fun, you know?'

I nodded. 'I know you do, Dave. You're a great dad, and he's a good kid. Happy, too, which is all that really matters.'

David ran a hand through his hair. 'To be honest, I never thought I would have my own family. But I love them so much, Jack. I didn't know I could love anyone so much.'

Seeing Dave made me realise I was the perfect person to take on this mission of Dr Lewis's. Dave would never have risked his son or Jessica for a chance at going back to the way things were. They were too important to him. But me? I had no future here; nothing and no one to protect other than mum, and she supported me wholeheartedly.

We stayed there for almost an hour, chatting nonsense, until I realised it was getting late.

'Haven't you got a family to get back to, Dave?'

'Yikes, time's getting on, isn't it? I'll see you around, mate. Try and get some sleep, yeah? You look like you need it!'

'I will, don't worry about me. Say hi to the family for me.'

'Will do,' Dave said, saluting like he was about to head off on a mission.

'You look after them, yeah? And yourself. You and Amy are like family to me, you know that, right?'

Dave nodded. He probably thought I was being sentimental because of Michael. Little did he know that I was the one about to leave on a mission.

I felt emotional saying goodbye to him, had felt it the whole way through our conversation. I think with everything going on, my emotions were a bit unbalanced. David was blissfully unaware this could be the last time we would see each other. The thought of that was heartbreaking, but I managed to keep my tears inside.

I couldn't let my fear influence my decision. I had to try to brush all that to one side and focus on the bigger picture.

I hoped that if I saw Dave after my venture into space, providing it went to plan, he'd be able to understand the situation I was in and we could continue our friendship where we'd left off. We had already gone through so many changes. The only constant in our lives was each other, and I just hoped our friendship would be able to survive one more change.

31

The next day, I felt a sense of optimism I hadn't felt in a long time. I had accepted whatever was going to happen. I would see Dr Lewis later, and I would tell him I was willing to go away with him. Today was the day.

I was so focused on my newfound determination that I didn't see Joe sprinting to catch up with me until he was right in front of me. He looked tired, downbeat. He gave my hand a firm shake, an intense look in his eyes.

'Jack, I just wanted to say... I'm just, I'm really sorry. For Michael, you know? *I'm* finding it hard, so I can only imagine how you feel. If you need anything, please let me know.'

Every word was said with perfect diction, as if it had been rehearsed. He was clearly grieving, but putting on a brave face for my benefit. I respected what he was trying to do; he was hurting too, but he wanted to be there for me.

I smiled and placed my hand on his shoulder, giving him permission to relax. It felt as if he dropped a couple of inches under the weight of my arm.

'Thanks, mate.'

'I was just hoping and praying it would all be okay. It's hard losing him. I just want you to know I'm here, that's all.' Joe was looking at the ground, embarrassed.

'Don't worry, Joe, you don't need to say anything. You're

a good friend, and a good person.' Despite being closer to Michael, I knew Joe needed the support too. 'Whatever happens, I'll be alright, I promise. And so will you.'

I knew I had said too much, but if I didn't return, I wanted to do what I could to avoid Joe worrying again. It was a subtle clue, but a clue nonetheless. I hoped that when I was gone, he would recall our conversation and know that I had something planned all along, giving him some sort of hope.

'What do you mean, whatever happens?'

I let out a puff of air, as if forcing out a laugh, trying to lighten the mood. 'Nothing, we just don't know what is round the corner, do we?'

We signed in with "Commander Wilson". It was almost funny, being the only one who knew this Elder was a fraud; that they all were. The Elders were the great pretenders; on the surface synchronised and in total control, but you didn't have to scratch too far below before the cracks started to appear. Undoubtedly more advanced than us, they were not better than us by any means, they had flaws just like we did. With my insider knowledge, my fear of them and respect for them had diminished. They were just another species after power and control, no matter how superior they acted.

I was thinking clearly and looking forward to my lesson later and seeing Dr Lewis. The sky was blue with lazy streaks of white splashed across it. Though there was a bit of cloud cover, it was still warm enough for the shorts and t-shirt I had opted to wear. I hadn't really considered how everyone else was feeling (they were all there for the announcement yesterday), but they weren't as close to Michael, nor did they know the truth about the Elders. I decided not to think about it, instead running with the positive and decisive mood I was in rather than falling back into the spiral of despair from which I had managed to escape.

As I walked to my lesson after our lunch break, I arrived at the exact same stretch where I had seen Dr Lewis eliminate Commander Wilson, and my good mood wavered. Unlike last time, the path was full of people heading into classrooms. Not a single clue remained from what happened. I walked down the pathway slowly and thoughtfully, reliving in my head the previous experience. I had a strange, indescribable feeling in the pit of my stomach, as if I was walking on hallowed ground. It didn't feel right, Michael not being here, nor did it feel right that no one along this path knew anything of what had happened here. A lot didn't feel right at that moment. I tried to keep my focus on what I *could* control: my breathing, heart rate, and keeping my head clear.

I stopped at the exact point where it had occurred. It was just a path, dust and dirt. There were no remains at all. There was no way anyone would have known or believed what I had seen. I continued walking – it was a short pathway, but felt longer than ever. I couldn't work out if I was nervous or excited. I felt a million times more anxious than I had on my first ever walk to school all those years ago. It was a new feeling, one I was not enjoying.

I arrived and slowly opened the door. The room was half-full. I looked at the scene in front of me and it felt like opening a door to my school days, groups of people huddled around tables chatting, waiting until the last minute to return to their own chairs for the lesson to begin. I went over to my desk at the front of the class and sat. Dr Lewis looked up at me and I nodded in acknowledgment. We both knew we would speak at the end of the lesson.

The lesson passed as normal. With only a few moments before I would be speaking to Dr Lewis, I had to switch my mind to the business at hand.

I stayed in my chair as everyone funnelled out of the door, people as eager to leave as I was for them to go, it seemed. It took a few minutes for the last person to walk out, shutting the door on their way. I had used those quiet moments at the end of the lesson wisely, getting myself ready, my posture relaxed as I sat back in my chair. We both remained silent. I was looking at Dr Lewis, who was examining sheets of paper in front of him, as if he had forgotten about our conversation.

'So, what's the plan?' I blurted out.

Dr Lewis looked up before simply replying, 'You know the plan, Jack.'

I nodded at him, pondering my next move. The last time we had spoken, I had been shaken and surprised, but this time I felt calmer, having used the intervening time to compose my thoughts.

'So, we are travelling to this other planet to try to convince some other alien race to come over and fight with us?'

'Yes.'

'Whom you cleverly named "The Rock Huggers"?

'Yes.'

I was like one of those nodding dog toys on the parcel shelf of a car. I focused, forcing myself to stop nodding. I leaned forward in my chair, resting my elbows against the desk in front of me.

'It's too simple. Is this really the best plan your intelligent species could come up with?'

'Sometimes the simplest plan can be the most effective.'

I probably hadn't given him enough credit; I was sure he must have been thinking about it for years, working out every possible option. The truth was, I trusted his judgment. If he thought this was the only way, then that was good enough for me.

I was nodding again. 'Okay.'

Silence filled the room. I still hadn't given Dr Lewis a definitive answer to whether I would be coming or not. It was like being in court when the lawyers gave their closing statements. Maybe something would be revealed to sway my decision.

'It's going to be dangerous, isn't it?' My voice came out quieter than I was expecting.

My nodding was obviously infectious as now Dr Lewis was doing it, his answer simple. 'There's no guarantee we will come back.'

I let out an exasperated sigh. I was acting cool, but I was still human; emotional. Dr Lewis was neither.

'It won't be easy either, will it?' I asked.

Disappointingly, Dr Lewis's nod turned into a shake. 'No, but is anything worth doing ever easy?'

I didn't rush my reply. Unlike Dr Lewis, who could have

been made from stone such was his passivity, my thoughts were etched all over my face. My lips curled inwards, my mouth slightly closed, eyebrows arched. The cogs in my head were spinning, trying to churn out a smart answer. A slight smile appeared on my face when I found my reply.

'Who was it who said it always seems impossible until it is done?'

'Nelson Mandela.'

I looked at him in disbelief. 'How did you know that?'

'We studied humans for hundreds of years. We know everything about you.'

'Of course.' I sighed loudly. 'And why should I trust you?'

'I've never lied to you, only hidden truths for your own safety.'

His answer was good, but had his reaction been more human, it would have been easier to trust him. The answers were so faultless and so quick, it almost seemed rehearsed, as if he was just saying the right thing automatically.

I looked him up and down, knowing it wasn't fair to judge him for being an Elder. Though he spoke like a robot, he had saved my life.

'You had better not be lying to me.'

'I have nothing to gain from lying to you, Jack. The only reason I shared this information with you was because I needed your help.'

'I mean, I am pretty great. I guess it's no surprise you need me,' I joked.

Predictably, Dr Lewis didn't so much as smirk. *Wrong audience.*

I squirmed uncomfortably in my chair and cleared my throat, brushing over my bad joke ad I quickly brought the conversation back to business. 'How long will it take?'

'Fifty days, to arrive at the planet. I don't know how long we will need to stay – it could take a day or months to state our case and persuade them to help. There is a small ship an hour and a half from here that we will be taking. Within fifteen minutes of entering it, you will be asleep. Travelling at the speed of light for such a long journey, and in a small space, can have severe repercussions. To prevent this, we fill the ships with toxins, keeping us unconscious throughout until we arrive.'

'Toxins?' I asked, nervous.

'Oh, you'll be quite safe.'

'But what if we're attacked along the way?'

'It's impossible to be attacked while travelling that fast.'

I didn't know if this was true or not but had no reason to doubt him.

I leant back in my chair, my fingers linked behind my head, my mind now made up. Rarely did destiny come calling at a convenient time, and I knew I had to answer the call. I was lucky – I had been given the opportunity to make a difference and do something worthwhile. I exhaled in readiness to say something, something that once it was released, there would be no way of taking back. I rocked my weight forward and leaned back on the table in preparation to deliver my verdict. I looked round the room just to make absolutely sure there was no one else who could hear what I was about to say. The school was empty now. It was just me, Dr Lewis and a very serious conversation.

'Okay, DL, I'm in,' I declared. 'When do we go?'

'Now.'

My eyes widened in shock. 'Excuse me?'

'We have no reason to wait, Jack. It isn't going to get any easier I'm afraid. You have had time to make up your mind, so I know it is not just a snap decision. I see no reason why we should delay.' Dr Lewis went over to his drawer as he spoke.

'Sorry, you just caught me by surprise. I didn't come here expecting to leave right away. You're saying we just leave this classroom, go to this ship and leave the planet?'

'Exactly. Now, take this.' Dr Lewis stretched out his arm to pass me an orb. I couldn't keep up with how fast everything was moving; it was becoming too unbelievable. 'It was Commander Wilson's,' he confirmed.

I took the orb and rolled it across my hand, inspecting it closely. I couldn't believe I was holding one of these. It was made from some kind of cold metal and was comfortable to hold, despite being heavier than it looked. I was completely silent, fixated on it. The orb was clean and shiny, like a mirror, and a disfigured version of me looked back at myself. I looked like an abstract painting with all my features stretched. I placed it on the table without taking my eyes off it. It didn't feel right having that much power in my hands. I never could have envisioned this. Every other time I had been this close to one, it had been pointed at me, my life in danger. I didn't know what to do with it; I had always been told it was too advanced for the human mind.

Now I was really panicking. 'I have no idea how to use

this, it's all too rushed, I'm not ready.'

'We are ready. We must leave now.'

Dr Lewis stood slowly and moved towards me decisively. I watched him, and before I knew it, I was looking up at him as he towered over me, his face immobile, his large, pitch-black, soulless eyes staring down at me, his large body blocking out the sun as it framed him in light. The Elders were an intimidating species, even Dr Lewis. I felt a shiver moving up my spine, either from nervous tension or the lack of sun now filtering through the window making me cold. Dr Lewis picked up the orb I had placed on the table and held it out to me in an open palm. I looked down at it as he spoke.

'The orb is only a precaution, Jack. The ships are never usually guarded – there is no reason for them to be, as we don't often fight each other.'

I leaned back to get a better view of his face and shook my head, still unconvinced I should be holding an orb. 'That's all well and good but I still don't know how to use it.'

'The technology supporting the orb is advanced, too advanced for you to ever comprehend. However, the orb itself is incredibly simple to use – it would be unnecessarily problematic if it wasn't. If the time comes when you must use the orb, simply aim it at the target and focus all your thoughts on it to fire. That is all you will need to do.'

'I don't know that I can,' I said, doubting myself. 'I'm only human.'

'And I am only an Elder. A human can use it; anyone who can focus their energy and thoughts can.'

'So, you believe I can do it?'

'I wouldn't have asked you if I didn't think you were ready. Now, are you coming or not?' Dr Lewis asked, pushing for an answer. There was no frustration in his tone as he pushed his hand forward one last time, the orb under my nose.

The talking was over; it was decision time. I knew I had to get it right.

I took a deep breath, adrenaline pumping around my body. I had never believed my life meant more than it did – I wasn't special – nor did I believe my life was building up to this moment. But right then, I felt significant, important; that I was about to do something momentous. I pushed my weight back, sliding my chair along with it. I sat tall and then stood even taller. I was only centimetres away from Dr Lewis, and though physically he was a lot taller and wider than me, right then I felt seven-foot tall, powerful, as if I could take on anything. I looked directly at him, as an equal, placing my hand on the orb he held out to me. I gripped it tightly and held it at my side, as if it had always been meant to be mine.

'I'm in.'

32

The decision had been made, there was no going back. I was to walk closely behind him and do exactly as he did, not to stop for anything unless instructed.

We made our way through the old school, a place I never thought I would leave. I had spent most of my childhood there, but now I was walking through it for what could be the last time. I thought of all the memories and friends I had made there; how it had felt the day we were all lined up waiting to be herded into groups, not knowing if we would live or die. These buildings had seen a lot over the years and were some of the few I knew of that had survived the invasion. Walking through the grounds, looking round at all the buildings, it was haunting, extracts of my life playing out in my head. I couldn't work out if I was happy or sad: the story of my post-invasion life.

We left the school and walked on for a moment before I turned to look at it one last time. Though built from bricks and mortar, these buildings symbolised the friends and family I was leaving behind. But I didn't have time to be sentimental and think about the life I had lived and the people I had met. There was a task at hand and I needed to focus.

I powered on, the route now unfamiliar – Dr Lewis knew a way out that would avoid other Elders. As soon as we crossed the district border, I would be without a stamp and thus a law breaker. I had never had any reason to head off in this direction before, and for the first half hour, we saw no one. But that didn't stop me feeling concerned and keeping my stamp-free arm as hidden as possible. There were clear paths to walk on, trees were dotted around. Thankfully, there was nothing we saw that looked out of the ordinary. It felt like an extended hike rather than a hero's mission.

Another half an hour passed; I was now in completely uncharted, unrecognisable territory. I might have known it in the past, but not anymore. Watchtowers were becoming increasingly less frequent, the trees dotted around becoming denser, thicker, taller. It was summertime, so they were covered in green leaves that acted like a thick blanket blocking out the little remaining sunshine. The paths were literally disappearing in front of my eyes, everything rural. It was becoming progressively more wooded, nature clearly the master this far out of town. I hadn't seen any life for a while; if Dr Lewis was leading me into a trap, this was the place to do it.

Everything seemed to be going smoothly.

Then I heard something.

Suddenly, I remembered the dangers out here, and my fear of the unknown grew.

'Go, go, go!' voices screamed.

They seemed angry, and from this distance, they sounded human.

Whoever it was, their voices carried well. I strained my eyes, looking all around, trying to spot anything I could.

I saw in the distance flashes of a person through the trees, reappearing every few seconds, sprinting in a straight line. He was either running to something, or away from it.

I turned in the direction he had come from and saw more people, ten, fifteen, all running in the same direction, like a pack of animals. They were a few hundred metres away and it was difficult to follow their movement through all the trees. Subconsciously, while watching them run, I edged closer to Dr Lewis, using him like a shield. I looked up at him, and saw his eyes were fixed on them.

'What's going on?' I whispered.

'Runners.'

'Runners?'

Without moving his gaze, he added, 'We don't see them very often anymore. They are trying to escape, but they won't get far. They never do.'

My eyes flickered between Dr Lewis and the runners, trying to think of something to do.

'We need to help them!' I said desperately.

'No,' Dr Lewis replied without hesitation. 'They can't escape. Not like that, anyway.'

'What do you mean?'

'Running, shouting. They will have been spotted a long time ago. That isn't the way to escape. Adrenaline and fear have taken over.'

'So, we just watch?'

Surely that wasn't the only option? We had to help. Wasn't that how a hero was meant to act? We were going on a journey to try to save the planet, yet we weren't capable of saving a handful of people.

'It's already over,' Dr Lewis said numbly.

Out of nowhere, the lead runner was vaporised by a bright light, and within seconds, lights were rapidly shooting through the trees, though I couldn't see where the lights were coming from.

I assumed it was the Elders firing their orbs and I was suddenly flooded by fear of what was out there and what could be watching us too. The overwhelming feeling of uselessness completely knocked my confidence. We watched the rest of the lightshow – just fifteen seconds long – the outcome as inevitable as Dr Lewis had predicted.

We stood in silence as I tried to process what I had just seen. I felt guilty that we hadn't done anything to help, then guilty for the relief I felt that we hadn't been spotted. I had to refocus: there was a task at hand, and nothing could distract us. We began moving and I scuttled off behind Dr Lewis sheepishly. I was frustrated and angered by my lack of action. I had been an onlooker, just watching people die. Here I was, pretending to be a hero, but I was merely a passenger. Dr Lewis was the one with a plan, calling the shots, trying to make a difference. I wasn't even his sidekick, just some mug he was taking along for the ride.

As we walked on, I couldn't help but keep reliving what I had seen, trying to figure out what I could have done differently to save them. I kept coming up short. I knew deep down that had I done anything, it would have threatened the mission, and I likely would have died too. Yet I couldn't help feeling guilty, like a fraud. What worried me the most was the fact I had frozen on the spot rather than reacting in any positive way. I didn't know what lay ahead, but what would happen if we were put in a position where I had to decide quickly and I didn't have Dr Lewis to help me? We would be in serious trouble.

I needed to shake this feeling and carry on. Whether I was purposely chosen, or had just been in the wrong place at the wrong time, it didn't matter. I was here now and needed to focus on my surroundings, no distractions.

I spent the next few moments clearing my mind.

The sky had turned a murky grey above the leaves; the sun had completely dropped out of the sky and wouldn't return until the morning. Luckily, my eyes had adjusted to the gradual fading light, but the visibility was now less than ideal. With all the trees and shrubbery in front of me, it was especially challenging trying to work out what was in the distance and plan ahead. My eyes were cruel, playing tricks on me; branches sticking out of the trees were beginning to look like the arms of Elders waiting for the right moment to strike. I had even managed to convince myself I had seen an Elder hiding behind a bush waiting to pounce. I was now keeping a keen eye on Dr Lewis – he was my only chance of staying safe if anything was to happen.

I had never done anything like this and didn't know the best tactic. I was trying to watch my step, making sure I knew where my foot was landing so as not to make a sound or to trip and injure myself. In addition, I was trying to look into the distance for dangers that may lay ahead.

Just over an hour had passed and we hadn't spoken for over half of it. It had never been Dr Lewis's habit to talk for the sake of talking, hence the long silence, but even if it had, I was too preoccupied with trying to stay alive to even want to speak.

He was just ahead of me when suddenly he stopped and stooped, as if he had spotted something. I stopped dead, immediately crouching, trying to keep in the safest position possible. I wasn't a hero and didn't feel brave; I was petrified. I looked up to see what Dr Lewis had spotted, praying it was nothing. He had already turned and noticed he had my attention. He nodded his head, pointing to a tree just in front of us. I was confused and didn't react as he moved silently towards it and beckoned me. I scrambled over, tucking in behind him in what I felt was the safest place possible.

'What is it?' I whispered, my eyes scanning the area, worried I had missed something obvious.

After a slight pause, Dr Lewis replied, 'Nothing yet. We are about fifteen minutes from the ship, but this is now getting deep into Elder territory. No human needs to be this far out, so if you are spotted, they will attack. Stay low and close behind me and keep a lookout for any movement. Stay ready. Stay prepared.'

'Okay.' I was already sceptical, but now I *really* doubted myself.

'Let's go.'

Dr Lewis edged forward and I followed extremely closely behind. I was hardly lifting my feet off the ground for fear of making a noise. The light had faded and we were now creatures of the night. We used the natural terrain as our cover, moving from tree to tree and staying low, moving smoothly and swiftly. Every snap of a branch or rustle of a leaf would send my blood pressure skyrocketing.

I was trying to walk with stealth but I was tense, stiff, walking clumsily in my panic, making the task difficult. If I saw something, how would I react? I was terrified I would panic and run, attracting attention to myself. I just needed to be calm, not a hindrance to Dr Lewis, and trust he knew what he was doing.

As we edged further and further into the unknown, I noticed an artificial light in the distance. It appeared to be coming from the ground. It was shining white and although it was still quite far away, it appeared to glow extremely brightly. Thankfully, Dr Lewis didn't seem startled by it. I assumed we were getting closer to our destination and that the light was coming from the ship.

'What's the light?' I enquired in a soft voice.

'It's the holding bay for the ships. It is illuminated so it can be easily spotted from the sky.'

I stared at the light in the distance, curious. 'Like a car park? You just leave them out there? Do you not have some fancy technology to keep them safe?'

'Yes, but it is unnecessary, Elders are not prisoners, we can move freely.'

Dr Lewis seemed so calm but this all seemed too convenient to me. 'But won't it be noticed that one is missing?'

Dr Lewis didn't take his eyes off his destination. 'Possibly, but it is of no concern. It is all part of the plan and will make sense.'

I found Dr Lewis' confidence comforting but my lack of knowledge disconcerting. I was part of the plan but not the planning process. Blind faith in an Elder had got me this far. It was unsettling, but negative thoughts wouldn't help me now.

We got closer to the light and everything was becoming clearer. I was no longer second guessing myself or having to strain my eyes; I could now easily see if there was any other life or danger out there. We stopped behind the final tree and knelt down. Ahead was flat, open land. I looked to my left and right. The trees had a slight bend inwards both ways to create a circle. They couldn't have grown like this naturally: a bald, circular patch of land in what was becoming overgrown forest. No, this had been made for a reason.

The space ahead of us was thirty metres in diameter and completely smooth, as if nothing had ever existed there. Whoever, or whatever, had removed the trees that once stood there, was a perfectionist. The lights on the ground were situated round the edge, a couple of metres apart from each other, facing inwards and illuminating the whole open space. Inside the space were four identical ships parked in a line in the middle. I had only ever seen two ships: the one Professor Watson had arrived in, and the one that engulfed the sky the night we were invaded. Despite this being the most dangerous and important situation of my life, for a second, I allowed myself to feel childlike excitement at seeing a spaceship.

'That's pretty cool,' I whispered, awestruck.

The ships were slick, silver and spotless. They were flat to the floor and looked like Professor Watson's ship, albeit a bit smaller. Each of them was compact, with smooth lines and a blacked-out windshield.

Dr Lewis stepped forward. 'That's how we are getting out of here, Jack.'

That's when I saw it: movement on the far-left side of the circle.

Instinctively I grabbed Dr Lewis's wrist and yanked him back. It was lucky I did, for two Elders walked into the circle.

Dr Lewis nodded gratefully at me; it felt good to get his approval. The two Elders stood in front of the ships, looking outwards. I felt uneasy. It was as if they were looking directly at us.

'What now?' I whispered. Had we come all this way for nothing? There was no cover so I didn't know what Dr Lewis would do. 'What are they doing?'

'They're guards, their job is to patrol the area and keep an eye on the ships. It is an informal arrangement; I was hoping we would be able to miss them entirely.' Dr Lewis didn't take his eyes off them.

'Can't we wait until they leave?' I asked, praying that would be the plan.

'No time. The longer we are out here, the greater the chance of finding trouble. They won't attack me. You wait here, I'll get closer.'

'What if they take you out, though? There are two of them. What would I do?'

'They won't take me out, because they won't see it coming. Trust me.'

I had never had reason to disbelieve Dr Lewis. He had obviously spent a long time thinking about the plan and would have anticipated this scenario. Elders didn't do anything on a whim, they were too logical.

'I wouldn't be here if I didn't trust you,' I said honestly, and for a moment, the irony and gravity of that statement hit me.

I really did trust him, an Elder, with my life and the lives of everyone I loved. We had one chance.

We had to get this right.

33

Dr Lewis walked casually, as though he didn't have a care in the world. His unsuspecting victims would have no idea that he was a rebel trying to bring down an entire movement. I was clearly doing the worrying for the both of us. The Elders guarding the ships wore black armbands like the ones I'd seen worn by the Elders who had stormed the canteen. I thought maybe the armband represented some sort of policing division. They barely acknowledged Dr Lewis (small talk was clearly not part of their culture). Indeed, with such a casual walk, it was difficult to comprehend he had a plan at all. I watched patiently, fearful something would go wrong.

Dr Lewis's attack was sudden. He fired two shots from his orb, instantly eliminating the Elder closest to him, who was blissfully unaware of what was going on. The shot didn't even have a chance to catch him by surprise, it was over so quickly.

The other Elder managed to evade the incoming shot, which went straight past him and destroyed a tree in the distance. In response, the remaining Elder retaliated, firing a shot back at Dr Lewis, who had thrown himself behind the ship to take cover.

It was now one-on-one, make or break. They were evenly matched; Dr Lewis had a fifty percent chance of winning the fight, great odds if he was playing poker but not so great for a fight to the death. Both Elders kept low, using the ships as cover, two predators hunting their prey, stalking each other, both strategically plotting and waiting for the right time to strike, neither giving the other an easy target to aim for. Although this dance had only been going on for a few seconds, it felt much longer. I couldn't envisage either of them slipping up to give their rival a chance to take the killer shot, they were both too competent.

I had front row seats to the most important showdown on Earth and not another being knew it was happening. I needed it to stay that way; I needed Dr Lewis to win. I was angry at myself for just sitting there, nothing more than a spectator. I shouldn't just be a passenger on Dr Lewis's ride. I was his partner, I needed to add value and be of assistance. But what could I do? He must have chosen me for a reason, and that reason couldn't simply be because I was a human. I had to tip the odds in his favour, somehow.

Think, Jack. I couldn't just step out as I would be shot dead within seconds. Instead, I put my hand into my pocket and carefully pulled out my orb. Could this be the solution? I didn't quite know how to use it, but I had to try.

I stared at it dejectedly. Dr Lewis said they were controlled by thoughts, but how on earth was I supposed to channel my thoughts into it? What did that even mean? It looked like a paperweight, or like some weird accessory someone would put on a coffee table and try to pass off as art. Maybe I would be better off just throwing it at the rival Elder? I had a good aim, and the orb was heavy enough to cause damage.

I looked up from the orb, plotting my next move, when I saw I had a clear shot. It didn't matter how stupid, ridiculous or underprepared I felt – the orb was my best chance of assisting Dr Lewis and tilting the battle in our favour. I stood tall and took a decisive step away from the safety of the trees. If the Elder turned around, they'd see me clearly; I prayed he was still too occupied with Dr Lewis to worry about the trees behind him. My arm lifted at a right angle, held rigid, and I pointed the orb directly at my target, trying to mirror the act of Elders I had seen in the past.

I had to focus all my energy on shooting. I did everything within my power to clear my mind, trying to forget the troubles of the last few days, trying to forget the seriousness of the situation, trying to forget anything that had ever happened to me. The only thing that mattered in this moment was firing the orb. All my thoughts were saying the same thing: *fire, fire, fire!*

Boom!

A burst of energy shot from the orb, bright blue, like a bolt of lightning, moving like a shooting star across the space. There was no recoil at all, my aim was perfect. The Elder vanished instantly upon being struck.

I lowered my arm in disbelief and exhaled a huge breath. I couldn't believe what I had done. I had killed an Elder; had made the first step to avenging humankind. I had always believed orbs to be too advanced for us to use; until just now, I had believed it impossible to do what I had just done. I stepped out confidently into the open and saw Dr Lewis's unharmed head pop up from above the farthest ship like a whack-a-mole. He raised his arm high above his head, giving me the thumbs up. It was a human gesture that they had learned: job well done.

I walked towards Dr Lewis with a mixture of pride and relief, still trembling, momentarily forgetting I was about to board a ship and leave Earth. I walked on, feeling like a hero, though I knew I hadn't saved the day yet.

This was only the beginning.

'Great shot, Jack, I knew you could do it. Thank you for saving me.' His voice, though as flat as ever, sounded grateful.

'No problem. Now we're even,' I answered boldly. 'I only wish I had one of these years ago.'

'You've got one to keep now.' Dr Lewis placed his hand flat on the side of the ship. He held it there for a few seconds before slowly pulling it away. An outline of a long, thin rectangle somehow appeared on the side where his hand had been. Then, a rectangle of metal disappeared, creating a door through which to enter.

'Spooky.'

'Let's go,' Dr Lewis said, stepping in.

I followed and sat next to him. There were four seats in the ship, two in the front where we sat and two directly behind. It was cosy and everything was black, simple, devoid of operational buttons. Simply four seats, each with a holder shaped like an eggcup, where the orbs were meant to sit, I assumed.

Dr Lewis placed his orb in the holder and I did the same, then the door we had entered through disappeared again. We weren't in darkness as the orbs glowed white, lighting up the ship. Dr Lewis projected a hologram, which filled the entire blacked out windshield. To me, the white-light hologram looked to be a picture of the night sky, with black dots representing stars in the distance. The picture then began moving and zoomed in on a section of the image, then a single star, and finally a planet adjacent to that star. The hologram then disappeared, and Dr Lewis's orb began to emit a bright green-light.

'What are you doing?' I asked, intrigued.

'Letting the ship know where we are going. The orb will do the rest,' he replied, removing his hand from the orb and onto his lap, then leaning back into his seat.

I felt a very slight movement beneath me as the ship left Earth. This was actually happening… we were in the air. Was it ever going to feel real?

It didn't help my nerves that the windshield was just for show. I couldn't see anything ahead of me, but I could sense we were speeding up.

'Are we travelling at the speed of light?' I asked, feeling a little nauseous. Travel sickness or regret, I couldn't be sure.

'Yes. We're now already well outside your solar system. Don't worry, we will both be asleep soon.' Dr Lewis was resting his head back, but still had his eyes wide open.

'No going back now, then,' I murmured, resting my own head back but opting to shut my eyes. Adrenaline was pumping all around my body, but I thought I might as well try to relax. I would be unconscious in a matter of minutes, anyway.

'No going back,' Dr Lewis confirmed.

As I sat there, getting drowsier and drowsier, I thought

about everyone and everything I was leaving behind. I thought about Claire and Dad and how, in many ways, I was doing this for them, even though they had been gone for such a long time. This wasn't a revenge mission, but I would be lying if I pretended it hadn't swayed my decision. I thought about David and his family, and how much I wanted to create a better life for them; for David's son. I thought about Mum and how heartbroken she was going to feel when she awoke tomorrow and realised I was gone, not knowing when or if she would see me again. The Elders would storm the canteen again, but this time, it wouldn't be Michael's face they'd be projecting. Would they search for Dr Lewis as well, or would he just be replaced, no questions asked, like Commander Wilson? I had so wanted to tell Amy, but I couldn't. Tomorrow, she would find out I was no longer there. I had to believe the mission would be successful and, one day in the future, I would have a chance to explain myself to her.

I thought about what could have been and how everything was now. I was getting worked up thinking about everyone I had left behind on Earth and how my decision would affect their lives, but I had to remind myself why I was doing this and not let the guilty feeling take over.

Despite the drowsiness starting to overcome me, my emotions still raged. I was overwhelmed and my eyes watered. There was a montage going on in my head of all the faces of people I loved and the memories I had created. I really hoped I would get to see them all again.

But for now, I had to focus on the plan.

My name is Jack Palmer, and three years ago, I was a young boy staring out of his classroom window, dreaming of adventure and freedom from my boring little life. Now, I'm on a journey to fight for it. I'm sitting next to an Elder, my partner, travelling through space at the speed of light, hoping to change the fate of humanity.

This isn't the end of my story, it's only the beginning.

The mission to save Earth starts now.

EPILOGUE

Do I regret what I did? No, I don't owe anybody anything, least of all an explanation. There were many times when I did doubt any of it was real, but regret? Not at all. If I died, what did it matter anyway? Time hadn't really existed since the invasion, not properly anyway. Day still followed night, but the days stopped meaning anything to me; I had stopped counting them.

I had lost track of how long I had been searching – weeks, months, I really didn't know nor care. I ate what I could find, slept when I got tired and just kept moving. My calves had grown tight, my shins were in constant pain and all my joints felt stiff and awkward. I had lost weight and was growing weaker by the day. I didn't know how much longer I would be able to travel for, but I would keep going until I no longer had the strength to lift my feet off the ground.

But then, it happened. I finally found it. The rumours were true.

I edged my way into the cave; it was completely silent except for the sound of my feet dragging through the puddles. The cave didn't seem habitable, no signs of life whatsoever, no reason for an Elder to ever be in here. I had been walking about five minutes, still no signs of life, and all the natural light had disappeared. However, surprisingly, there were lights above that let out a dull glow every ten metres.

I finally reached the red door. I leaned up against it and, with my last ounce of strength, knocked on it. I inhaled slowly. I wasn't scared, I was exhausted. I heard footsteps getting louder and louder as they moved closer to the door, then dead silence. Eyes then appeared from the viewing window on the door, and I heard the words I had been dreaming about hearing for as long as I knew about its existence. It was what had kept me going.

'Welcome to the Resistance, Michael.'

ACKNOWLEDGMENTS

Thank you for taking the time to read my story.

The Jack Palmer journey started many years ago, when I was in my early twenties, and it wouldn't be a published book without the help and support of many people along the way.

I had the idea many years ago and took my time completing the first draft. As someone who is dyslexic, I knew it needed a good look at by someone who would do so without judgement. I owe my partner, Natalie, a huge thank you, not only for reading it and checking the many spelling mistakes while fitting it around work and life, but for always believing in it. Thank you for everything!

Next, both my parents and brother, Chris, kindly read and checked it, again without judgement. I owe Chris a big thanks for the best review it will get: "it's a lot better than I thought it would be". I am very lucky to have a supportive family who were willing to give up time and effort, thank you.

Once the manuscript was completed and ready to send out, I was not prepared, at all, for the process of finding a publisher, and quickly became lost on the internet with no idea where to look. Without the advice of "KevDog" from Natalie's school, I never would have found a publisher. So a big thank you Kev!

I owe everyone at Cranthorpe Millner a huge thank you for giving a dyslexic teacher a chance! Victoria and Becca, thank you for always answering any question I've had, being so supportive and giving advice with such kindness. Michelle and Kirsty, thank you for all your support with editing, I am so proud of the final outcome and that is because of your hard work.

I'd like to thank all my friends for their support, whether it be as simple as posting about Jack Palmer, sharing it with friends and family or just letting me go on about it the whole time, which I know can be relentless! A particular thanks to Scott, for helping with (saving) the website; Jim, for taking the time to create concept art for the website; Neil, Matt and James for helping with events, and Rick for helping with the printing of marketing material.

I owe a big thank you to anyone I have asked a favour of over the last year. This whole experience has shown me how kind and supportive people can be. I hope you all enjoyed it!

Finally, to any child I have taught over the years who has had the opportunity to read *A New Order*. I hope you enjoyed it and it gives you the belief that if you have an idea, anything is possible, regardless how old you are. Or, at the very least, I hope it gives you the confidence to give it a try!